THE DEPUTY AND THE SINGLE MOM

Sierra Mountain Deputies

MARIA MICHAELS

*To my children Tyler, Danielle, and Brandon.
God's greatest gifts to me.*

Chapter 1

The first sound that filtered into Jack Butler's ears was the whimper of Tim Whitman's little boy as he cried out for his father. Something inside Jack shifted, and only then did he relax his grip on the man's neck. A thought began to form but froze immediately as his heart raced ahead.

"Get off him! Now!" Jack heard Sheriff Calhoun's words as though they came out of a wind tunnel.

Get it together, Jack. Snap out of it. Now.

He knew what he had to do, but men like Tim Whitman didn't help.

Tim's face was contorted in a snarl, and he stared at Jack like a pit bull about to pounce. Jack wanted to warn him that the last man to look at him that way had ended on his stomach in handcuffs, but that was more than a year ago. And he wasn't a U.S. Marshal any longer.

Red faced, Tim rubbed his neck. "Did you see that? He tried to kill me!"

"You're fine," Jack said as he took a slow deep breath the way the doctor in Virginia had recommended.

Deep breaths. As many as it takes. I'll be fine.

"I'll have your badge, you lunatic!" Tim stumbled, bracing himself against the front door.

The scent of gun powder competed with the strong scent of whiskey. Jack shook his head. The whiskey scent was happening now, and the gun powder was only a memory. He wasn't in Virginia; he was in California, and Tim didn't have a gun in his hands even though he was a bully. Jack hated a bully.

"Let's all calm down. From where I stood, Tim, you shoved my deputy. That was an assault on my officer."

Sheriff Calhoun stood between them and spoke in even, measured tones, one arm extended toward Jack and the other toward Tim.

"Yeah? We'll see if a court of law sees it the same way." Tim threw open the ornate front door of his sprawling mansion and slammed it behind him.

Next time I'll throw the guy on the ground and give him a taste of his own medicine. I'm in trouble anyway.

Jack and Sheriff Calhoun were responding to a disturbance call made by Mrs. Mock, who lived next door to the Whitman family. When they arrived, Tim had shoved Jack. Mistake number one.

Calhoun gave him the thousand-yard stare. "You know, the biggest problem we've had today was you, Jack. Get it together."

"I don't care if he's a big time attorney. He's a mean drunk. I'm not surprised a man who defends rapists and murderers would knock his wife around."

When he'd stepped between Tim and his wife, the last thing Jack clearly recalled was being shoved. After that, everything else faded into the pounding of blood in his eardrums as he grabbed Tim by the collar and pushed him up against his front door.

Calhoun glared at Jack. "You let me do the talking now."

Jack took several paces back to stand by the cruiser as Calhoun knocked on the door and spoke with Mrs. Whitman again. She was a petite, dark-haired woman with frightened eyes. He'd seen those eyes before. Like those of a wounded animal, seeking cover. Behind her, in the shadows, for the first time Jack noticed a teenaged boy standing to her right.

And even though the air appeared to be calm for the moment, Jack stayed alert, resting his hand on his Glock. He'd seen these situations turn in an instant. But try telling that to a Sheriff who had ruled a small town where the worst of the criminals were two faced men like Tim Wright. Calhoun believed in the best of everyone, and from the way he smiled as he spoke with Mrs. Whitman they could have been talking about the weather.

It might also take Jack thirty years on the job to have that kind of peace while walking through the messes that people made of their lives, but he hoped not. He didn't have that kind of time, not if he wanted to get back home to Virginia where he belonged.

Calhoun handed her a card, and she glanced behind her before she took it. Another tell-tale sign. The woman was terrified of her husband. She closed the front door, and Calhoun ambled back to the cruiser.

"She said it was her fault, and it won't happen again," Calhoun said.

Jack shook his head. "What a load of—"

"Enough, son. We'll talk about this when we get back to the station."

"Sorry, but I can't apologize. How many times have we been out here? The man is a menace. Not only does he make a mockery out of the justice system, he terrorizes his wife and kids. When he makes it home from his media appearances."

Tim Whitman was a high profile criminal defense attorney probably only interested in making money, along with a sprinkle or two of fame. Jack had personally witnessed attorneys like Tim defend the indefensible and unravel months of tedious police work.

They drove outside the entryway of the gated community, where the most economically privileged in Harte's Peak resided, and toward downtown and the tiny sheriff's office nestled between the store fronts on Main

Street. Not for the first time, he gazed in awe of the tall pine trees surrounding them. Sometimes, if he timed it right, the view could calm him. He breathed in now, as his heartbeat slowed to its normal rhythm.

Harte's Peak had turned out to be the perfect place to hide. He'd read that in the 1950s a small group of communists intent on overthrowing the government had holed up in a cabin in Harte's Peak while on the run from the FBI. An interesting bit of trivia he'd found hidden in a small book about the history of the town. The small resort town prided itself on its reputation as being the gateway to the Sierras and the town's lake was a majestic beauty. Only a fifteen-mile drive away in the nearby town of Pinecrest stood one of the top ranked ski resorts in the country.

Right or wrong, he'd wound up here after taking a leave from the U.S. Marshals service six months ago.

"'A fool gives full vent to his spirit, but a wise man quietly holds it back.' Proverbs 29:11. Have you ever heard that before, Jack?" Calhoun interrupted his thoughts.

Not again. Calhoun was a religious man who gave Jack a Bible his first week on the job. "I can't say that I have, but then again, I'm no altar boy."

Religion was fine for some people, but it was a crutch he didn't need. So he lost his temper every now and then, but at home in Virginia, no one had ever faulted him for getting a bit hotheaded at times. If the sheriff had walked in his shoes for one day, he would have bet money he'd now be using that Bible as a paperweight.

"You can say that again. Listen, this tough guy façade will only get you so far. I understand your frustration, but you need to let the system work."

Oh, that was a rich one. Let the system work. Well, he'd tried that over the last ten years, and so far, he couldn't see that the system did much but serve as a revolving door.

"And in the meantime what are we supposed to do? Should I have let him punch his wife right in front of us?"

Calhoun shook his head. "I'm not saying that, but maybe there was something you could have done between that and nearly strangling the man."

He'd done no such thing, but recognized this was yet another battle he would not win.

He closed his eyes and pinched the bridge of his nose. "You're right. It won't happen again."

"No, it won't." Calhoun said. "I'll make sure of that, son."

"That sounds ominous."

"It's not. I've been praying for you. And I won't stop until you've forgiven yourself."

Jack tensed. He didn't like when Calhoun brought up forgiveness. Calhoun was one of only two people in town who knew Jack's past—all of it. And by now he should realize forgiveness wouldn't happen anytime soon, so Calhoun might just wear out his knees.

"Son, if you don't think I wanted to do the same to Whitman, then you don't know me. It's just that I've learned over the years how to hold my temper. I couldn't have done it without the help of the good Lord." He patted the Bible he kept on the dashboard of his cruiser.

Jack did not want to hear the religious stuff, but he also didn't want to offend Calhoun. The man ran a youth group, and it didn't hurt that he looked a little like Santa Claus with his hefty build and white beard. Everybody in town loved him. He probably couldn't help the fact that he had a ridiculously sunny and rather unrealistic disposition.

But then again, Calhoun hadn't seen the things Jack had. Calhoun didn't have to live with the memories that made their way into Jack's dreams every night.

"You're not going to ask me to go to church again, are you?"

"Well, that's a standing offer. Any time you're ready, the Lord will be there."

Jack sighed. In some ways, that's what he was afraid of the most. He had a lot of good to do to make up for what he'd done, and today probably hadn't helped his accounting in heaven.

___

JACK PULLED into the driveway of his rented home on Twain Harte Drive. The mature elm trees in desperate need of pruning lined the cul-de-sac, and an abundance of cars were parked on the street of Harte's Peak's oldest middle class neighborhood. It turned out that the modest cottage was the only place he could find that would accept a month to month lease.

After today's incident, Calhoun had sent him home early and ordered him to get some rest. *Rest. What a joke.* He did need a nap, hopefully followed by a good night's sleep, though he doubted he would get either.

What he definitely didn't need was what he witnessed as he shut his truck off. A figure, pressed against the front window of his neighbor's house two doors down, clearly pushing the window open from the outside.

Entering through the front window in broad daylight.

Great. Will this day never end?

From the brand name skateboarding shoes and the matching logo t-shirt, the intruder could be a kid, and that was the last thing he wanted to deal with right now. Kids were unpredictable, dangerous. But no way would an intruder get away with a B&E. Not in his neighborhood. The people on this street couldn't have much, so what was this kid after? Probably a TV set or the latest PlayStation.

He approached the front of his neighbor's house, hand resting on his weapon just in case the uniform wasn't enough to send the kid running. He'd let this one go as long as the kid didn't make it in the house, no harm done. Things were different in Harte's Peak, not like back home in Virginia. This was a small community and even the kids were normally well behaved. Just his luck to run into a troublemaker.

It didn't help that he wasn't even sure who lived in the house or if they were at home, since he'd made it a point not to meet any of his neighbors.

A few words indicating that he lived next door should send the kid running and that would be the end of it. He'd go inside, grab a soda, and stare at the empty walls, maybe watch the game until it was time for his next shift. The work was what he lived for nowadays. It kept him grounded, rooted. As long as he had work, he had a reason to stay alive.

He approached the house with slow, sure steps and watched the kid hang one leg over the windowsill, oblivious to his approach. Not exactly a professional. This might be the kid's first foray into stealing.

"Can I help you?" he asked the kid in his deepest and loudest tone.

The kid startled, and when she turned her face to him, he realized it was a teenaged girl. She squealed her surprise, lost her balance, and promptly fell inside through the window.

Super. Officially breaking and entering—or more like breaking and falling. He edged to the window, looked down at the display, and assessed that she wasn't hurt. He didn't see any bleeding or scratches, but she lay splayed across the floor in a heap, her dark brown hair forming a cloud around her head.

"Are you OK, kid?"

He pushed down the panic in his voice. *Please. No more kids hurt on my watch.*

"I'm fine! And I didn't do anything wrong." She pushed hair out of her equally dark brown eyes. Raised her chin, defiant. Nice. So it was his fault he'd caught her in the act.

"Except breaking and entering." He took a deep breath in and let it out.

"What did you say?" The kid seemed confused.

Maybe she had a concussion.

"Get up. I'll take you to the station, and we can call your parents."

The last thing he wanted to do was be responsible for this kid, but she'd committed a crime right in front of his eyes, and he couldn't let her go now. Knowing Sheriff Calhoun and his bleeding heart ways, he'd probably just give the girl a stern lecture.

"My parents? Why? Are you nuts?"

"No, but maybe you are. Then again, you probably didn't realize a cop lives in this neighborhood. You picked the wrong house, kid."

His voice sounded strained in his ears. The breathing exercises weren't working. Again. He just wanted to get away from here and go back in his house where he could breathe. Why did this kid have to pick his neighborhood?

"I live here, you nerd." She almost spat the words out, scrambling to her feet.

He was supposed to believe that.

"The front door is a better place to come in if you live here. And you can come out the front door now. I'm guessing the owners aren't home."

"You don't believe me. Gee, what a shock."

"Why should I?"

In his experience, best relegated to the deep recesses of his mind, kids rarely told the truth. He used to believe them as much as he believed anyone else, until he'd been burned.

"I can call my mother. She'll tell you." Her defiance continued, unabated. This kid was a piece of work.

"You better do that."

He would have to talk to the kid's mother anyway. Might as well have her come to him, and then they could all three drive to the station. He'd let Calhoun decide what to do with the kid.

The girl reached inside her jeans pocket for a cell phone. He watched as she pushed buttons and sighed with exasperation.

"No luck?"

"She never remembers to turn her phone off silent."

Jack shrugged. He'd bet this kid had a million excuses, and maybe there was no mother coming at all.

ONE YEAR AGO, Maggie Bradshaw could only operate her own coffeemaker, but now she churned out one drink after another. Espressos, lattés, and chai to plain drip, and she had the recipes memorized. Not that she poured coffee from a pot often, but when she had an order like that, she stopped for a moment and took a deep breath.

Her favorites were the iced drinks, and during afternoon lulls she experimented with flavors and mixes. Vera Carrington, her boss and the owner of The Bean, loved Maggie's creativity and even encouraged it. She even named one of the drinks that Maggie had concocted after her: Maggie's Marvelous Mysterious Mocha. It contained the secret ingredients—specialty chocolate mixed with just a hint of cherry.

"Taste this."

Maggie handed Vera a small sample of her newest blend, a mixture of coconut and hazelnut.

Vera stopped sweeping the floor. "Yum, you've done it again. Put that one on the menu, too."

"It's not quite ready. There's something missing, but I'll figure it out. I just need to play around some more with the flavors."

The doorbell dinged announcing a new customer had walked in.

"Well, not now. Lover Boy is here again and there's no way I'm dealing with him today." Vera turned her back.

Ryan Colton was by far Harte's Peak

most eligible bachelor, and one of Vera's biggest fans. On the other hand, also a big fan of every woman. And with his rugged good looks, it was no wonder most women were part of the I Want to Date Ryan Fan Club. Not Vera, though. A mystery Maggie could still not crack.

"The usual, Ryan?" Maggie made preparations for a double espresso.

"Please don't tell me I'm that pre-dictable, or I'll have to change my order," Ryan said as he fiddled with the straws and seemed to ignore Vera.

Vera did a good job of ignoring him as well, staying near the back. They'd nearly made ignoring each other a spectator sport.

Vera, whose dating life was practically a *Who's Who* in Harte's County, had somehow decided that Ryan was off limits to her. Go figure.

"Here you go, Ryan."

She slid him the espresso with a tentative smile. She didn't like playing this silly game. These two needed to realize they were crazy about each other and get over it.

"Are you girls obeying the speed limit like you promised you would?" Ryan asked with a boyish smile.

Maggie noticed that Vera threw him a look but didn't respond. They both knew he meant Vera, who accumulated a speeding ticket every other week.

"Obeying the speed limit is what I do." Maggie put a hand to her chest. "And I'm good at it."

"You make my day," Ryan said.

The phone rang, and Vera rushed to get it.

"Maggie, get over here," she called out.

But the phone couldn't possibly be for her. Lexi always called the cellphone, and who else could it be? Strolling toward the back where the phone was located, Maggie smiled.

"Finally ready to talk to him?"

"I'm serious. It's Lexi, and she sounds upset."

Vera handed her the phone. Maggie fished inside her apron for the cellphone she kept near for emergencies. There were three missed calls on it from Lexi. Maggie had forgotten to take the phone off silent. Again.

"Mom, some stupid cop wants to arrest me." Lexi's voice sounded small and tiny over the phone.

"What? Where are you?"

"I'm at home. Only he doesn't believe me."

A number of questions popped in Maggie's head, like why Lexi hadn't walked to the café after school as she usually did, but there would be time for that later.

"I'll be right there."

Maggie hung up the phone, and grabbed her purse and keys. "Vera, I have to go. Lexi is—"

"Go! Tell me about it later."

Maggie ran past Ryan, hopped in her vehicle, and prayed it would start on the first try this time. She had to get home immediately, because there obviously had to be some mistake. Of course, she would just straighten this out, and they would laugh about it later. For all the trouble she'd caused in the past year, Lexi had never become acquainted with law enforcement.

What could she have done at their own home to cause the police to come after her?

Please, God. I need You now. It's just You and me.

Why is this happening?

Maybe she really wasn't cut out to be a mother because the evidence so far was that she had failed.

Since their move to Harte's Peak, Lexi's behavior had gone from bad to worse, with rolling eyes and loud sighs a new way of communication. Just last week her algebra teacher caught her cheating on a test. The two of them should be able to get through this difficult time.

Lexi was hurting and acting out. What could she have done at their own home to cause the police to come after her?

Please, God. I need You now. It's just You and me.

Why is this happening?

Maybe she really wasn't cut out to be a mother because the evidence so far was that she had failed.

Since their move to Harte's Peak, Lexi's behavior had gone from bad to worse, with rolling eyes and loud sighs a new way of communication. Just last week her algebra teacher caught her cheating on a test. The two of them should be able to get through this difficult time. Lexi was hurting and acting out. Maggie knew that, but she had no idea how to help her.

Lexi had pulled away from 'those church kids,' as she called them, as if she knew she didn't belong. It was a constant struggle every Sunday to get her out the door and to church on time, and any attempt at affection toward Lexi left Maggie feeling like she'd hugged a cactus.

If only Matt were here. He'd know what to do. But Matt was never coming home again, and they'd both have to get used to that.

Chapter 2

According to his watch, Jack had waited five minutes, which his constricted chest made seem more like five hours, when a silver SUV peeled into the driveway and a petite woman emerged, panic etched on every angle of her porcelain-like face. Long, wild strawberry blonde hair fell in waves around her face, and her eyes were the color of the pine trees that covered the mountains of Harte's Peak. He'd heard the kid tell her mother to come without giving her any directions, so this appeared to be a huge misunderstanding.

"What happened?" The woman asked and jarred him out of his daydream.

"Is this your daughter?" He pointed to

the kid, who now sat on the porch with anger blazing in her eyes.

"Yes, this is my daughter Lexi. I'm Maggie Bradshaw. What on earth happened?" She was out of breath.

Jack had scared her for no good reason.

"Officer Jack Butler. There's been a mistake. I saw your daughter climbing through the front window, and I assumed she was breaking and entering."

He couldn't shake the feeling that he was almost as relieved as she was that it was all a big mistake.

"You know you're supposed to meet me at the cafe after school." Maggie glanced at her daughter.

"I'm tired of being treated like a baby. I want to come home and do my homework, not sit at the cafe so you can keep your eye on me. If you would leave me a key, this wouldn't have happened." The kid pouted.

"I'm so sorry, Officer. It won't happen again," Maggie said.

"I'm the one who's sorry. I shouldn't have jumped to conclusions but…"

He felt like an idiot, but he was doing his job. He wasn't a mind reader, and he hadn't exactly been at the top of his game. No, not for some time.

"That's right!" Lexi interrupted.

"Lexi, he was just trying to help."

Maggie defended him, and his mind briefly flashed back to Virginia and the parent of another teen. If that parent had helped law enforcement, her kid would be fine today.

Stop it, Butler. It's your fault. Don't blame anyone else.

"Well, now will you leave me a key so I can stop looking like a criminal?" Lexi stood and put her hands on her hips.

"You and I will talk about that. Later." Maggie shot her daughter a pleading look and then turned her attention back to him. "Thanks for watching over our neighborhood. You never know. It could have been a real burglar."

Exactly. "I live two doors down."

He hooked his thumb in the direction of his house.

He didn't know why he thought it was important that she realize that. He usually liked to keep a low profile and had managed to avoid his neighbors so far. Let someone know a cop lived next door and suddenly every minor neighborhood issue was a matter for law enforcement. But he also didn't want Maggie to think he randomly drove by neighborhoods mistakenly arresting people who were locked out of their homes.

"So you're the new neighbor. I've been meaning to come by and welcome you to the neighborhood. I've been busy." Maggie smiled for the first time, the sweetness in her eyes mimicking the upward curve of her lips.

He decided she should do that more often. Or, maybe less, at least around him. The last thing he needed right now was to be distracted by a beautiful married woman. He'd surely rack up extra points in heaven for that one. Right.

Keep your eyes where they belong, Butler.

Of course, she would be busy with a kid like Lexi. Now he wondered about Mr. Bradshaw, not that it was any of his business. "I'm not home much. Work crazy shifts. But thanks."

"Is it OK if I go inside my own house now?" Lexi's arms were crossed over her chest, eyes bulging out of their sockets.

For a second he thought smoke might come out of her nose.

Maggie nodded and the kid stomped inside but not before shooting another hateful glare in his direction. *Good job, Butler. Making friends again.*

"I apologize for my daughter. She's thirteen going on thirty, and we've been butting heads lately." She bit her lower lip.

He wasn't equipped to dispense advice on raising kids. "What does her dad say about it?"

Maggie blinked. "Oh, he—he's not around. But in answer to your question, he would probably not like this much at all."

Jack would bet his life on it. "Again, I'm sorry if I upset you."

"Please don't apologize. It's nice to know we have a deputy in the neighborhood."

"I promise not to arrest either of you for locking yourselves out of the house." It was an effort at lightheartedness that fell flat, though Maggie was too kind not to laugh.

"Believe me. It won't happen again." Maggie nodded and put her hand on the door knob.

"Well if it does, you don't have to worry about me."

He would mind his own business from now on if it killed him, as long as no crimes were being committed. Trying to help a kid hadn't worked once before, and this sure wasn't working out too well now.

Although for once he wouldn't mind being a bit neighborly if Maggie were doing the asking.

As long as the requests had nothing to do with her daughter.

———

MAGGIE LEANED against the front door and shut her eyes for a second, trying to get the image of her handsome neighbor out of her mind and pull it back to her wayward teen.

It used to be so much easier in the days when I could bandage a cut and make it all better with a kiss. Lord, I need Your help.

Until today life had been calm on the home front for the past week, without any calls from Lexi's frustrated teachers. It gave her a sense of hope that maybe the bad times were finally in the past. And now this.

Thank God it had been a big misunderstanding.

She couldn't cope with one more thing going wrong.

At the same time as she railed against her lack of freedom, Lexi constantly demonstrated why she didn't deserve it. But, somehow, Maggie couldn't get that across to her thirteen-year-old, no matter how hard she tried. Now she lay deep in the middle of another parenting conundrum. If she gave Lexi a key now, she'd be rewarding bad behavior.

Maggie glanced down and realized she still wore her café apron, a splatter of chocolate stains all over it. *Great first impression.* He must think you're mother of the year. Maggie sighed.

Cops should only be that good looking on television. Jack Butler had a build that showed he spent time at the gym and light brown closed-cropped hair that set off his steel blue eyes. A good thing that she'd resolved not to date until Lexi was grown, because the deputy was precisely the kind of man that made her heart skip.

But her mission was to be a good mother, and she would not fail at it.

Parenting Lexi on her own had so far been much harder than she'd ever imagined. She needed help, but the last time she'd let someone render assistance, they'd almost taken everything from her. That would never happen again.

And then the seed of an idea germinated in her mind. Whether she realized it or not, Lexi needed the presence of an adult man in her life, and Maggie wouldn't be dating anytime soon. She had to concentrate on her daughter and easing the pain of losing her father.

Jack had asked about Lexi's father, but as usual, Maggie couldn't even say the words out loud. *Matt is never coming home.*

She walked into the small and crowded kitchen where she found a simmered down Lexi at the table, her textbook open. She had a boxed juice drink in front of her and had pulled the bowl of grapes out of the fridge.

Maggie gazed at her daughter's profile only to feel a hitch in her breath when, for a second, Lexi looked just like Matt, her lips pursed as she concentrated, holding the pencil in her left hand.

Having Lexi was like having Matt with her all the time, reminding her that she'd better do a good job and not ruin the best, maybe the only, good thing they'd ever done together.

She sat down across from Lexi at the same stained and marked table she and Matt had owned since the early days of their marriage. Lexi had colored on this table since the time she could hold a crayon in her hand.

"I'm going back to work, but first I want to talk to you."

"What now?" Lexi met her eyes as though it took a Herculean effort.

Maggie sat down next to her. "First things first. You were rude to Officer Butler. I want you to apologize to him."

"Apologize? To him? He thought I broke into my own house."

"He apologized for his mistake. You didn't have to be so short with him."

"What can I say? I didn't want to stand there and watch you flirt with him." Lexi rolled her eyes.

Maggie closed her eyes and counted to ten. Lexi always knew what buttons to push, and if Maggie didn't make the offer soon, Lexi would talk her way right out of it.

"I've decided to give you a key, and please don't make me regret it."

Lexi's eyes brightened, and she dropped her pencil. "Really?"

"But it's not because of what happened today. It's in spite of what happened today. I feel safer knowing we live near a cop, and now I want to give you the chance to prove to me that you can be responsible."

She prayed she wouldn't come to regret this decision, like so many others.

"Great. Are you going to have him spy on me now?" Lexi's eyes narrowed into slits.

"Of course not. He has an important job to do, and it's not to babysit you."

Not babysit, but guide, lift up, encourage. That's what she hoped for, anyway.

"That's good, because I don't need a babysitter." Lexi frowned.

They'd have to set a few ground rules, and she'd make sure they were enforced. It would help to have another set of eyes at least some of the time. She only hoped the officer didn't mind the intrusion, because right now she desperately needed his help.

If she didn't get control of Lexi soon, she could risk losing her all over again.

———

THE BEAUTIFUL MESS of a woman who lived two doors down was that rare woman he heard about often but never met in real life: a woman who appeared to be unaware of her own beauty. Legend held that there were women like that in the world, but until now, Jack had not believed it to be true.

She had obviously dropped everything when her daughter called, evidenced by the black apron from The Bean. That was a first. Most parents he'd dealt with in the past came in red faced and ready to tear right into their kid. And then him, for having the nerve to catch their little darlings doing something wrong.

He was thinking about Maggie's long and wavy hair when his doorbell rang, causing him to startle and instinctively grab his Glock. *Calm down.* He'd just moved in recently, and even Ryan Colton, his best friend and fellow deputy, had yet to drop by.

Mostly because Jack liked to keep to himself, even though it went against doctor's orders. Those orders were to reconnect with society, understand the inherent good in people, and a lot of other nonsense he'd already forgotten.

He peered at his new neighbor through the keyhole. *Maggie.* Even the name was beautiful and rolled off the tongue like an

Irish melody, and surely the Big Guy didn't mind him looking a bit now since Mr. Bradshaw was out of the picture. No, still not a good idea. Single mom and all that, and the kid was a deal breaker.

He opened the door with his cell phone in hand, so maybe she'd think she interrupted him in the middle of something important. That usually did the trick. Act busy and maybe they'll leave faster.

"Can I help you?"

"I'm sorry to interrupt. May I speak to you for a few minutes?"

He'd be willing to talk to her for hours, but there was the matter of the kid. "Come in."

She brushed by him, a coconut scent in her strawberry blonde hair leaving a trail in his wake. He swallowed hard.

"Sorry, I don't have any furniture yet. I haven't had much free time since I moved in." Best to keep busy, he'd found, since it left so much less time for thinking.

There were two seats in his kitchen—one of them a milk carton and the other a stool. He offered her the stool as he leaned against the kitchen counter.

"This won't take long," Maggie said.

And for some odd reason, that didn't make him feel better. "So what's up?"

She looked at the floor and didn't meet his eyes, so either she was uncomfortable or had just committed a crime. He settled on the former.

"It's Lexi. She's been difficult since we moved here. I don't know what to do anymore."

"Is she skipping school? Hanging out with a bad crowd?"

He wouldn't be surprised, since kids from single parent households were at a higher risk.

Maggie's green eyes widened. "No. I hope not. She's had some problems at school, but I want to make sure things don't get any worse. She just needs a little guidance."

Good idea, but what did it have to do with him?

"There are some programs at the county level. I'm not sure, but I could look into it for you..."

Maggie smiled with a longing in her eyes that made his chest tighten.

"I hoped you would help personally. You're our neighbor. We always taught Lexi to trust law enforcement. You could talk to her sometime, and tell her how important it is to stay on the straight and narrow."

Anything but that. He didn't want to be around kids. They were too unpredictable. And tragic. "Thing is though, I'm uh—not great with kids."

Quite possibly the understatement of the year, buddy.

"You've never had any of your own?" He shook his head. "Nope."

"I wouldn't say Lexi is the easiest kid to get along with, but she really is a good kid once you get to know her." Spoken from the mouth of a hopeful mother.

"I'm sure she is." He was not sure of any such thing.

"Lexi needs a positive male role model in her life. She and her dad were so close." Her eyes darkened.

Nice. Another absentee father. "So there's no one else—no uncle, grandfather?"

At the mention of grandfather, he didn't imagine it when she visibly tensed. Definitely something going on there.

"Grandfather, yes, but he's a busy attorney here in town."

"It sounds like he just needs to re-prioritize." Attorneys often had that problem. Take Tim, for example.

She stared at him. "Please. Just talk to her."

Every muscle in his body tensed. He wanted to help with clogged sinks, jump-starting cars, maybe even killing a spider or two. Why couldn't she have asked him for anything but this?

"But—"

"I don't know what I'm going to do with her. She's not the girl she used to be. She talks back, skipped class once, cheated on a test at school, and she doesn't ever want to go to church anymore." Maggie wrung her hands.

He couldn't blame the kid about church. Who wanted to be dragged into a building every Sunday with all the other hypocrites? And as for the few sincere people, religion was just another crutch.

Of course, he would put Maggie in that latter group, which only made him worry about her. Did she go around asking complete strangers for help? What if she ran into the wrong person?

"I don't know why you're asking me. You don't even know me." There. He'd said it out loud, even if it felt like he'd just kicked a puppy.

It didn't seem to faze her. "My brother is a police officer in Colorado, and I have a good sense about people. There's a little bit of good in everyone, and my instincts are dead on."

Jack cleared his throat. "What does your brother say about this instinct of yours?"

Maggie shrugged. "Well, he doesn't count. He's a bit overprotective. Actually, he might yell at me if I asked anyone else, but I know he'd trust another police officer."

She'd picked the one person who couldn't help her. Wearing a law enforcement uniform didn't make him a good person. Yeah, sure, he tried and failed miserably every day, but he certainly didn't want to tell her that.

He stared at those green eyes, the trembling rosebud lips. *Look away, Butler.*

But his lips moved as though independent of the brain that knew better. "Sure. I'll have a talk with her sometime."

The sweat dripped down his back. A real excuse would mean explaining what had happened in Virginia, and that's the last thing he wanted to do.

Chapter 3

Jack pulled into the Harte's Peak YMCA parking lot in his long-bed pickup and hoped for once Ryan wouldn't be late. They met on the basketball courts every other Saturday for pick-up games with a group that had assembled a couple of years ago and included a handful of cops and firefighters from all over the county. Basketball was one of the few things that calmed him these days.

Ryan would brag about his latest female conquest, when the only thing on Jack's mind was how he could get out of the arrangement he had agreed to with Maggie. Maggie with the emerald eyes. She'd just asked him to do the unthinkable. *Mentor a teenager.*

From what he had witnessed so far, Ryan managed to weasel out of most commitments. Maybe he had some advice Jack could use.

Maggie deserved a better man to mentor her daughter, certainly someone who could sleep through the night without waking up in a cold sweat. Someone who hadn't messed up as badly as he had.

Ryan pulled in right beside him, uncharacteristically on time. They greeted each other and walked in to the gym together.

"How do you like the new place?" Ryan asked.

"Funny you should mention that."

"Why?" Ryan set his gym bag down and pulled out a water bottle.

"I have a problem with my neighbor." Jack threw Ryan his basketball, and they began to play a little one- on-one before the others trickled in.

"Already?" Ryan whistled. "Hoo boy, Butler, you do have a way with people, don't you?"

"Not that kind of problem."

Jack scored a shot that would have easily been a three pointer if they were keeping score. Too bad they weren't, because Ryan needed to be schooled.

"Are you going to tell me or what?" Ryan asked, taking the rebound.

"It's my neighbor. She asked me to mentor her teenaged daughter."

"So what's the big deal?"

"You know the big deal."

Ryan and their boss, Sheriff Calhoun, were the only two who knew what had happened in Virginia. And he planned to keep it that way.

Ryan stopped mid-dribble and stared at Jack. "It's like ripping off a bandage. You need to get over it."

Easier said than done. He wasn't ready yet, and the way he was going, he might never be.

Jack scored another three-pointer. Where were the guys anyway? If Ryan wouldn't help him, they might as well start this game and stop talking. He wanted to start scoring.

Ryan roughly grabbed the rebound. Perhaps they were keeping score. "If you don't want to help, then just tell her no. What's the big deal?"

"She needs help. You should meet her

kid, a real piece of work. And the dad is not in the picture."

"Yeah? So what's this neighbor's name?" Ryan pressed, dunking the ball.

"Maggie Bradshaw."

Ryan stopped under the basket, and whistled.

"*Maggie Bradshaw?* Well, now it all makes sense."

"What does?" Jack asked.

"I see why you won't say no to her. But fair warning. Sure she's gorgeous, but she's the ice queen of Harte's County." Ryan laughed. "She and her daughter came back about a year ago to live near her in-laws. She's a widow."

A widow. He felt worse for Maggie, and if it were possible, even a little sorry for Lexi. Losing a loved one wasn't easy on a kid, or a grown man, for that matter.

"Before you get any ideas, I asked her out a few months ago, and she turned me down flat. Know what she said? 'I don't date.' Those were her exact words. So good luck with that," Ryan said.

"Sure thing, buddy, but did it ever occur to you that she just doesn't want to date the town's Romeo?" Jack asked.

"Oh, you are dead!" Ryan fouled Jack, almost knocking him to the ground.

Jack gained his bearings quickly to make the next shot. *Just get over it.* Hadn't that been what he'd tried to do for the past year? And even though he'd finally quit the Marshals Service and moved three thousand miles away, he'd brought the nightmares with him.

———

THANK YOU, *Lord.* For the first time in a year, Maggie woke up with the thought that the tide had turned in her favor. She had a law enforcement official who would talk some sense into her daughter. He'd agreed to do it, anyway. But the way they'd left things she still wasn't sure how they would make it work. She couldn't just bring Lexi over to him for a lecture. That might be a little too obvious.

Maybe now she would get some real help with Lexi, not the pseudo-support of a grandfather and grandmother who couldn't find fault with anything their only granddaughter did.

Richard and Paula Bradshaw did not seem to understand that giving Lexi material things would not fill the hole in her heart that her father's death had left. She'd agreed to move back to Harte's Peak, the small town where she and Matt were both raised, because her in-laws promised to help them adjust after Matt's death. Instead, they'd plotted against her, and she still struggled to forgive them for the pain they'd caused. The Lord was helping her with that, but progress was slow.

The last thing she wanted them to know was that she was having trouble with Lexi, especially if their absence was a big part of the problem. They already believed that she could not adequately parent Matt's child.

If only Mom were still alive.

Maggie's mother had managed as a single mother, and so could she. Maggie hadn't been given any choice in the matter, but even so, she believed God had a plan for her future. She just had to hold on and trust in God, and keep putting one foot in front of the other.

Holding her mug of steaming coffee, Maggie gazed out the bay window of her kitchen. Up in the mountains, the air might be thinner, but for the first time in almost a year, she breathed a deep sigh of relief.

Small reminders of winter remained in the patches of snow not yet melted away, but spring began to debut in its own immortal way. Daffodil bulbs were already pushing through, little sprigs of green. A reminder that life goes on.

The landscape changed as a white pickup pulled into the neighbor's driveway and Jack emerged, carrying a basketball. Off duty, he dressed in basketball shorts and a white sports shirt that couldn't hide his athletic arms and well defined chest. *He plays basketball. Lexi and Matt used to play basketball.*

"Mom!" Lexi screeched from the family room, and Maggie startled.

So much for quietly enjoying the landscape of beautiful things. She sighed and turned away from the window.

"What is it?" She walked into the family room where Lexi sat at the desktop computer.

"It's doing it again. This computer is a dinosaur. That's what Grandpa says," Lexi whined. "It doesn't have the bandwidth I need."

She'd been begging for a new computer, but it wasn't in their budget, and the way things were going it might not be for some time.

"I don't care what Grandpa says. This computer is all I can afford." She motioned for Lexi to move and sat down to figure out the problem. "You have homework on a Saturday?"

"It's a special project for my Photoshop class."

"Did you try restarting it yet?"

"Yes, and it's still slow. And you don't have to buy me a new computer. Grandpa says he'll buy me a laptop, and I can take it everywhere I go. Even in my bedroom."

"No. We've talked about this, and you can't have a computer in your bedroom."

"Great, Mom. Why do you have to ruin everything for me?" Lexi stomped out of the room.

Apparently, it had never occurred to Richard that a teenager should not have un-restricted access to the Internet.

Maggie sighed and restarted it again. When that didn't help, she restarted it a second time and resisted the urge to kick the thing. A blue screen appeared and informed her that she'd just completed a fatal error.

Wonderful. Another item to add to the

ever growing list of things she couldn't afford. Working at the café with Vera was a great job, but her salary wasn't anything to get excited about.

During her marriage, she'd never worked outside of the home. Never even started working on the college degree she'd always meant to obtain. Matt was a teacher, and though they didn't have much money, he supported Maggie's desire to stay home and raise their daughter. The plan was for her to return to school for her own degree once Lexi entered high school. But those plans, like so much else, were lost. Maybe forever.

She glanced at the clock. There was still time to drive Lexi over to the small county library to use the computer, but the last time the computer had frozen up this way they'd waited in line for two hours to use one of the three computers available.

On the other hand, her neighbor probably had a working computer. Didn't almost everyone else in the state except for her? Surely he'd be eager to help, and it would give him a chance to have a few encouraging words with Lexi.

Nothing like the Lord's perfect timing.

She knocked on Lexi's bedroom door

and entered to find Lexi on her bed, a scowl on her face, ear buds in her ears. "We're going over to see our new neighbor."

JACK HAD JUST GOTTEN out of the shower and grabbed a pair of jeans when he heard the doorbell. Again. Two days in a row. It probably wasn't Ryan, and he hoped it wasn't Maggie again. He pulled on a t-shirt and went to the front door where he looked through the eyehole.

Maggie stood on the other side of his door, and the kid was with her. Presumably, with a few well-chosen words, he could magically straighten her out. Right. He hadn't even had time to think of what he would say since he'd been so busy trying to think of a way out.

Guess that will teach me.

He opened the door to a smiling Maggie and a pouting Lexi.

"Hi."

He hesitated asking them inside. Maggie was welcome, but the kid not so much. Lexi pierced him with hate filled eyes, clearing up the fact that the feeling was mutual.

"Lexi wanted to say something to you." Maggie turned to her daughter.

Lexi sighed. "Sorry I was rude. You were just doing your job." The glare in her eyes showed him she believed no such thing.

"Apology accepted. Well, it's a warm day, and I'm sure you both have a lot to do." He started to close the door.

Lexi took the hint and almost leapt back to her house. Maggie's gaze followed her for a moment, but she stayed planted in front of his door.

"Is there something else?" *Please say no.*

"I know it's asking a lot, but—" Maggie said.

"It's OK. I said I'd talk to her and I will." He was about to add that he wanted more time when she interrupted him.

"It's not that, it's just that we have computer problems."

"What kind of problems?" He was no computer expert, but maybe he could help. This was more of what he had in mind in the first place.

"The kind of problems you have when you own a dinosaur, according to my daughter." She lifted a shoulder.

He had a perfectly good desktop computer he only used to check e-mail, since he had access to state of the art software at work. Maybe if he gave them the computer, all would be forgotten. He would have done his part. Surely, Maggie would see the sense in that.

"You can have mine." He would check his e-mail at work from now on.

She blinked. "I'm sorry?"

"You can have my computer. I don't use it all that often. The little time I'm home I eat and sleep."

Or tried to sleep. More like lay awake and watched the neon green numbers on his alarm clock turn.

She laughed and tossed that wavy hair. "I couldn't do that. That's very generous of you."

Generous or cowardly? "It's nothing."

"Although, if you wouldn't mind, it would be great if Lexi could come here and borrow your computer for a little bit. She's got a project for her photography class, and I think our computer just died. I haven't told her yet, but I may have to break down and buy one soon. But for now, until I save up enough money, your offer is accepted."

Offer? He hadn't offered to bring the kid

into his home. He'd given up his computer, a clear signal that he'd do almost anything to avoid having her in his house. Apparently, Maggie-Rose-Colored-Glasses wasn't getting his hints.

"But I was going to…" His mind sought an excuse but came up with nothing.

"This would give you a chance to just say a few encouraging words." Maggie smiled and his resolve crumbled.

After all, he'd agreed to that. "Uh, sure."

"We can come over anytime that's good for you. I hope it would only take her an hour or so to get her project done."

"I'll be home most of the day."

He fastened onto the 'we' in Maggie's words. No way would he allow a teenage girl in his home—especially one with Lexi's attitude—without a parent present. However, something about Maggie's presence and the soft lilt of her voice soothed his jangled nerves like nothing else.

"I'll ask Lexi, but we should be over just after lunch."

At least he'd have some time to figure out what he could possibly say to a teenage girl that would make any sense.

He closed the door and immediately

began straightening up his family room. The computer was in there, along with moving boxes, which lined the walls. The unpacked boxes reassured him that this was all temporary, and soon enough he'd be back in Virginia with the Marshals, this entire experience nothing but a memory.

Except that now the boxes, the bare walls and sparse furnishings sat in judgment. What would his neighbor think? He'd moved in a month ago and still hadn't settled in. Often the same kind of behavior he'd witnessed from the fugitives he pursued.

For the next hour, he worked like a fiend and lined up all the boxes in his bedroom instead, which he should have thought of sooner. Maybe the reassuring presence and reminder that soon he'd be back in Virginia would help him get a good-night's sleep tonight. Might as well try that, since he was starting to get desperate.

He went over a mini-lecture that he'd give to Lexi. Something he'd heard mentioned in the Marshals' youth programs. Stuff about responsibility, caring for others, selflessness, appreciation. Although how he'd fit it all in one brief talk was beyond him.

His experience was speaking to prisoners in short, clipped sentences.

Don't move. Show me hands. You have the right to remain silent…

He should probably call Calhoun and ask for advice, but Maggie hadn't even given him any time to do that. Probably he should have thought of that first before going to Ryan, who, as usual, was of no help to Jack whatsoever. If he thought about it now, he was pretty sure Calhoun had mentioned something about a youth group. He made a mental note to ask him.

Now that he lived near a single mother and her troubled teen, he was supposed to be some kind of expert. Right. Everyone who knew him realized that his skills didn't go much beyond ordering kids around. Fortunately, most of them listened, unlike Lexi.

If there was a God, and Jack still doubted that, He had some kind of wicked sense of humor. Jack had traveled almost three thousand miles from Virginia only to wind up living close to a teenager. And if her mom had any idea how badly he'd messed up with the last teenager he'd tried to help, she might not be so anxious for his help.

True to her word, Maggie was back with Lexi within a short hour.

He'd barely had enough time to more the boxes and straighten up the place.

She carried a plastic-wrapped plate of something that looked like lasagna. "I brought you some lunch in case you haven't eaten yet."

Maggie placed the covered plate in his hands.

His stomach growled since he'd forgotten to eat again. "That wasn't necessary, but thanks."

He showed Lexi to the computer in the family room and heard her foot stomps behind him. She wasn't any happier about this than he was. After he'd installed the software she handed him, he stood and allowed her to sit in the chair.

Maggie exchanged a few pleasantries with him before she said something that jerked him back to reality. "I think I forgot to turn off the oven. Be right back."

"Hurry up, Mom. You're going to burn the house down one day," Lexi quipped.

He followed Maggie out the door.

Once outside, she turned to him and smiled. "I'll just be right back. This will give you a few minutes to talk to her. Is that OK?"

"Of course, but what do you want me to tell her, exactly?" He should have thought of this sooner. Why not go to the source?

"Maybe something encouraging. Uplifting. I trust you can think of something."

She practically skipped next door, no doubt thinking about unicorns and rainbows.

"Sure."

No pressure. He'd think of something. Right. He walked back to the living room, and although he was no scientist, he would swear that there was suddenly far less oxygen in the room.

The panic started as it always did, rising up from somewhere beneath his chest and spreading until every cell in his body sat on edge. Maybe if he just stood and watched her, he could keep her out of harm's way. He leaned against the wall.

Lexi glared. "I'm not a baby. You can go do whatever you have to do. You don't need to watch me."

Yeah, a likely story. Turn your back on a teen, and you may as well turn your back on the ocean.

He took a breath. "Your mother wants me to talk to you."

Lexi gave a deep sigh accompanied by a well- practiced eye roll.

"What a surprise. Let me help you out. There's nothing wrong with me other than I have a wicked controlling mother."

Jack didn't think her controlling enough, but he kept quiet. In his silence, she kept going.

"Once you get to know my mom you'll see she overreacts to everything. I guess because she grew up like some kind of angel in a Hallmark card. But I'm different. I'm like my dad."

She raised her chin, a hint of pride in her dark eyes.

"But—"

"So you can spare me your speech on how important it is to stay in school, stay away from drugs, don't accept rides from strangers, listen to your mother, and go to church." She held one finger in the air with every item she recited.

"That's pretty good."

She'd covered almost everything he thought about for close to two hours, other than church. In some ways, this kid was impressive.

"It's not like I haven't heard it all a gazillion times before." She shrugged.

Although, apparently, all the advice wasn't getting through to her. He'd done his job and could now try to relax a little. He picked up the plate of lasagna he'd placed on the desk.

"And since you're being nice enough to let me borrow your computer, I'll clue you in on a few things, too. First of all, my mom is not as great as you think she is."

"What makes you think…?" he protested. Great, the kid had noticed the interest he thought he'd disguised.

Lexi held up a hand. "Save it. For one thing, she's controlling. I don't think guys like that. Second, she's a Jesus freak. And lastly, and most important to you, my mother can't cook. *At all.*"

She glanced at the plate of food in his hands.

He'd been looking forward to the lasagna and wondered if the kid was messing with him. Anyone could see she wasn't her mother's greatest advocate, not to mention kids were picky eaters, last he'd heard. And there was also the fact that he was starving.

"But you're welcome to try." She said with a smirk.

One thing for sure, he was hungry enough to take his chances. The lasagna was still warm as he carried it into the kitchen, grabbed a clean fork from the dishwasher and took a large bite. It was then that he discovered that Lexi Bradshaw might be a lot of things—precocious, smart, hostile—but she was certainly no liar.

Chapter 4

Maggie hummed as she dipped carafes in the sudsy water.

"You've been perky all morning. Want to tell me why?" Vera asked.

"I've got some good news. That's all."

"So go ahead and spill it. What's going on?" Vera cocked her head to one side.

"I met my new neighbor, and he's a cop. He seems nice, and he agreed to talk to Lexi."

"You're letting a perfect stranger talk to Lexi? What's wrong with you? Who *is* this guy?"

"Only one of Harte's Peak's finest." In more ways than one, she had to admit.

"What did happen with Lexi? You ran out of here so fast I never found out."

"That's a funny story."

Funny in hindsight, anyway. In a few minutes, she'd explained the whole mess to Vera.

"I know all the deputies since they've each written me at least one speeding ticket. Which one is it?" Vera wiped the counter while they experienced their afternoon lull.

"Jack Butler."

"Butler?" Vera stopped wiping.

"Yes, why?" Maggie asked.

"Nothing, he's come in here before with Ryan." Vera rolled her eyes, her standard response when saying Ryan's name. "Well, Jack is all right. For a cop. He was pretty polite when he wrote me up for a ticket last week. Lots of integrity. He wouldn't budge, despite my flirting. Handsome, too, don't you think?"

Maggie's cheeks burned. Leave it to Vera to have that be her first thought. "I hadn't noticed. He's just helping me hopefully straighten Lexi out. Anyway, you know I can't date right now."

It was different for Vera, and not just because she was blonde, tall, and thin and looked like she should still be on a runway somewhere in Paris instead of the owner of a small town café.

"Your daughter is practically grown. And you can take care of Lexi, but who'll take care of you?" Vera asked.

Good question. "I guess I'll have to take care of myself right now."

"That's no fun."

"I wouldn't even have any idea how to act on a date. The last time I went out with someone, I'd just gotten my license. What do people do on dates these days?" Maggie was only half-kidding.

"Please, you sound like you're sixty years old instead of thirty-one. You have a lot of life left to live."

"I know. I just don't know if Lexi will be OK with me living it."

"Who's the parent?" Vera crossed her arms.

Maggie sighed. Vera didn't understand because she'd never been a parent or experienced putting herself last. Or even second.

"This is how you do it. You go out on a date and put the guy through his paces. Date him awhile, and if he's good material, then you allow him to meet the kid." Vera spoke as though she were an expert on the subject.

She made it sound so easy, but Maggie had met Matt in high school. When he'd asked her out the first time, she didn't answer because the bell rang for fourth period and she didn't want to be late. Their romance was short -lived since she'd gotten pregnant with Lexi in her senior year, and both she and Matt left their youth behind at an early age.

"How do *you* know this stuff?" Maggie asked.

"Learned it from my sister, after she divorced her husband. It worked out fine, too. You're a rookie, but I'll help you out." Vera flashed her runway model smile.

The difference was that Maggie had not divorced her husband, and even with all their problems, she doubted she ever would have. "Thanks, but I'm sure he's not interested in me. Even if I was interested in him. Which I'm not."

"Whatever you say, Mags."

Of course, Maggie had noticed his looks, but relationships were about so much more than that. Still. *OK, so the man is a hunk.* But a man was the last thing on her mind.

Vera wanted Maggie to get out there, start meeting people, live her life. But she was doing that now, finally reconnecting with her daughter, and readjusting her new definition of a family. It would be just the two of them now. The two of them and the Lord.

She certainly couldn't count on Lexi's grandparents anymore, even if they'd been the entire reason she'd moved back to California.

Maggie's cell phone rang, and she pulled it from her apron pocket. As she viewed the caller ID, her heart sank. "Vera, I'm taking a quick break."

"Maggie? Is that you?"

Paula Bradshaw's voice still grated on Maggie's nerves. *Please Lord, help me to be kinder. I know that I have to forgive her, and I already have. But it doesn't mean I have to like her, does it?*

"Of course it's me, Paula."

"We haven't seen Lexi in two weeks. We're the grandparents, or did you forget? Really, Maggie, must you be so selfish?"

"We've been busy." Maggie wondered how long that excuse would satisfy them. Her guess was not much longer.

"We worry when we don't hear from you."

"You don't have to worry. We're fine."

She could take care of her own daughter and resented Paula's implication that there was anything to worry about.

There was a pause on the other end of the line.

"You say that now, but less than a year ago…"

Maggie cut her off. "I'm not interested in rehashing the past."

"But we meant well. You were such a mess. And Lexi needs us, whether you like it or not."

Paula didn't know when to quit.

Seconds from hanging up on her, Maggie counted to twenty and remembered that Paula meant well and adored her only grandchild.

"Why don't you come by tomorrow after church? But I'd like Richard to stay away. For now."

"But what should I tell Richard?"

Maggie had a lot she personally wanted to tell Richard. Like the fact that he would never be able to hurt Lexi the way he'd hurt

Matt. Not if Maggie had anything to do with it.

"Tell him he can talk to Lexi over the phone. And ask him to stop mentioning the laptop. I won't let Lexi have unrestricted access to the Internet."

"Richard was just trying to help. You have so many rules to follow."

"I'm her mother, in case you forgot."

She liked to refresh their memory every now and then because they seemed to need the reminder.

"We know that." Paula sighed. "Thank you, Maggie. I'll be over tomorrow in the afternoon."

Maggie had been talking to her pastor about it for weeks, and it was time to give a little. Trusting them again would be a battle, but she had to step out in faith. Her trust was now fully in the Lord, and he required her forgiveness.

Except that the thought of how they'd betrayed her at her weakest moment would be impossible to ever forget.

▭

THE NIGHTMARES RETURNED with the little sleep he managed, and even though the dreams hardly made sense, Jack still woke up in a cold sweat. This time he made his way across a mud filled lake, and on the other side was his old partner, U.S. Marshal Robert Craig.

Jack knew instinctively how vital it was to reach the other side of the lake while the boy stood next to Craig saying nothing, a smirk on his face. Just inches from his destination, Jack lost his footing and fell into a deep crevice. His head under water, he struggled to swim in the dense, sludge-filled water while the boy's laughter echoed around him.

The nightmares were his reward for finally getting some sleep. More than once, he'd picked up the bottle of sleeping pills and opened it. Stared inside to make sure the pills were still there. Then he closed the top again.

And now for the first time in weeks, he dialed the number for Bridget Logan, his doctor in Virginia. She asked how he was doing, and he pictured her short salt and pepper hair and probing dark eyes.

I'm not doing OK. I'm drowning. Someone throw me a line.

But he never gave voice to the thoughts any more than he had months ago when he sat across from her, and she'd pinned him with her stare.

"Fine. Still have trouble sleeping."

She paused a moment. "The pills will help with that, but something tells me you haven't taken any of them."

Sleep without nightmares would be even better. If only they had a pill for that.

He heard the rustling of a paper on the other end of the line. "Have you found a new therapist yet?"

"Not yet. Still looking. This is a small town." He rubbed his forehead, where the headache was starting.

"There's nothing more I can do for you. I hate doing this, but I have to close your file. It's important that you talk to someone. You need to find another therapist. As I've already explained PTSD is not something you can just—"

"Good talking to you, doctor." Jack cut her off in mid-sentence and hung up the phone.

His state of mind was just fine, although his attention span considerably worsened every time he was near Maggie. The problem was sleep. Somewhere he'd read that a man could exist on four hours of sleep a night as long as it was restful REM sleep. Of course, the article never said a man would be at his best on four hours a night, or what that man should do if he was plagued by constant nightmares.

Logan might have gone to school for ten years, and she had fancy diplomas on her wall, but no matter what she said, she didn't know what it was like to know that two people were dead because of you.

He'd pulled another shift from Ryan who had taken a girl away for the weekend. As soon as he could leave and stop staring at the four walls, he'd stop thinking about the bad cook next door. The beautiful one with green eyes and coconut-smelling hair. The one with the smart-alecky teenager he was supposed to somehow rescue. Yeah, right.

He would be paired with Sheriff Calhoun, so he'd take the opportunity to ask him about those youth programs. Then maybe Maggie would be happy and leave him alone. He'd done what he could with

Lexi. She wouldn't exactly listen to him, and neither did he want to keep trying.

Fortunately for Jack, Calhoun was always in a pious mood on a Sunday because he hated to miss church. If Jack played his cards right, he'd have Calhoun taking his place and mentoring Lexi. He'd probably welcome the challenge.

After checking in with dispatch, Calhoun and Jack took the cruiser out. If Harte's Peak was quiet on a normal day, Sunday gave new meaning to the word monotonous.

"How's the new place?" Calhoun asked.

Just like that, the door was opened, and Jack walked right in. In a few minutes, he'd explained the entire situation to Calhoun.

"The Bradshaws? I know them. They're part of my church family." Calhoun frowned. "I knew something was going on there. Lexi always seems so unhappy."

"You heard her dad passed away?"

"Yes, and they've been on our prayer chain many times. It was rough there for a while."

"I thought maybe you could tell me of a good program for her. I could let Maggie know where she can find help."

Then he could be off the hook. He was

so close now he could almost smell and taste freedom.

"Program? The only programs I know are for kids far worse off than Lexi. No, Lexi will be OK. She's got a good mother. A good, solid foundation."

"I agree, but Maggie thinks she needs the influence of a father-type figure."

Right about now he wondered why that man couldn't be Calhoun. Sure, he'd be more like a grandfather, but perfect for the job. Jack opened his mouth to suggest it when Calhoun interrupted him.

"I've always said the Lord works in mysterious ways." Calhoun said with a glance at Jack and a twinkle in his eyes.

The twinkle in the eyes, the beard, the ruddy cheeks. Santa Claus. Only Jack didn't want the present he'd brought. "What's that supposed to mean?"

"It means this is the perfect opportunity for you to work out your fear."

There was that word again, and said aloud, it made his stomach tense. He didn't want to believe he was afraid of anything. He didn't operate that way.

"You know I hate that word."

"Whatever you want to call it, but it's

time to move on, son. And this girl could use your help. What'll it hurt to have a few conversations with her?"

It would hurt a lot, but that wasn't the point.

"There have to be other people who would be better at this than me."

"But that's why God put you there. Those other people don't need to learn this particular lesson."

He could see he wouldn't get any support from Calhoun. Not the man who told him he would not be put into any situation he could not work through with the Lord.

"I don't want to learn any lessons. I moved into your sister's rental because I couldn't live in a motel anymore. There's only one apartment complex in town, and her house was the only place that would take a month-to-month lease."

Calhoun laughed. "I know, and look where it got you. From the frying pan into the fire. Perfect."

"I don't have any idea what to say to this girl. And she's not exactly the easiest person in the world to talk to."

Of course, Maggie was a different story, but Calhoun didn't need to know about that.

"Son, no teenager is. But something tells me you'll find a way."

Jack sighed, realizing he was on his own. If Dr. Logan was to be believed, and he'd have to face his greatest fear in order to sleep a full night again, then he was now on his way. If only the thought of it didn't make him cringe.

ONE THING you could say about Harte's Peak— endless beauty surrounded the town —from the pine trees cradling its boundaries to the woman sitting on her front porch as he pulled into his driveway.

Maggie sat on the wrought iron bench and stared into the distance at nothing in particular. When she caught him looking at her through the window of his truck, she waved.

He jerked like a deer caught in the headlights because somehow it seemed wrong to walk inside his house now and ignore her smiling face. Even if that was safer. He walked over, hands in his pockets.

"Hi," he offered.

Butler, stop acting like you've never talked to a woman before.

"Just getting off work?"

"Yep." Another one word sentence slipped out.

"I hope you don't always have to work on Sundays." Her green eyes were sympathetic, and he only wished he deserved it.

"I told you I work crazy hours." A succulent smell emanated from her home, and he wondered if they were having take-out. "Whatever you're cooking, it sure smells good."

Maggie didn't appear particularly happy to hear it for some odd reason.

He shifted gears. "I talked to Lexi."

"She told me." Her eyes lit up. "I can't tell you how much I appreciate it. She said you told her everything she needed to know."

Uh-oh. He'd done nothing of the sort and couldn't find words again.

An older woman with short and wavy salt and pepper hair poked her head out the open front door.

"Maggie, the fried chicken is ready. Oh, hello." She glanced at Jack, her eyes scanning the uniform and then turned to Maggie again. "Is anything wrong?"

"No," Maggie answered immediately. "This is my neighbor, Jack Butler. Jack, this is my mother-in-law, Paula Bradshaw. Lexi's grandma."

Jack stuck his hand out and shook Paula's. "Nice to meet you."

"Maybe you'd like some fried chicken, too. It's Lexi's favorite, and I made plenty," Paula said.

His perpetually empty stomach almost spoke for him, but the dejected expression in Maggie's eyes kept him from accepting. Somehow, he realized that would make her unhappy, though why, he couldn't hazard a guess.

"No, thanks, ma'am. I'm fine."

"I'll be there in a minute," Maggie said to Paula, who shut the door again.

He stole another glance at Maggie. Her arms were folded in front of her in a defensive posture. Obviously, something bothered her, though he would think she should be glad to have the help with her obnoxious teen. If it were him, he'd take a long drive and reconsider coming back.

"Well, you all have a good dinner."

Turning, he started to walk next door. He wanted to get inside and away from this strange feeling, different from his normal hunger pangs, roiling around in the pit of his stomach.

"How did you like my lasagna?" Maggie asked, and he turned back to face her.

"It was delicious," he lied.

Her smile was so genuine that for the first time in months Jack felt something stir inside the cold place he used to call his heart.

"Thanks. Lexi doesn't like my cooking for some reason. Paula's a great cook. In fact, she's pretty much great at everything." She shrugged.

He recognized that look because it was one he saw in the mirror every day. Resigned, defeated, worthless. No way would he let Maggie feel that way about herself.

"I meant to tell you. Lexi is…"

He didn't know where he was going with this. Flying by the seat of his pants maybe, but no more lies. "A very smart girl. You've done a great job."

The kid was smart all right, since she seemed to be two steps ahead of her mom.

"Thank you. Her dad was the real brains in the family. I think she takes after him."

She certainly didn't take after her sweet mother.

"That's what she told me."

"She did? What did she say?" Maggie asked.

Leaving the kid's snide comments about Maggie out, he repeated what Lexi had told him about her father.

"She's right. I guess it would be boring if she was just like me." Maggie caught the silver lining.

"Good point."

"I better get inside. Paula likes it when we eat dinner together." She turned toward the door.

Jack walked back to his quiet home, wondering what kind of canned food he'd open up and heat tonight. He was getting used to this hermit-like existence although a nagging thought he wanted to ignore reminded him it might not be a good thing.

Ryan was forever trying to fix him up on a date, and he'd refused every time. He didn't even like the thought of talking to anyone, much less buying a dinner and sitting through it. Better not start up anything he couldn't finish.

After all, he would return to Virginia and the Marshals as soon as he got the insomnia and the nightmares under control. That had been the plan all along. Out here in the boondocks, he might not have to be at the top of his game to function, but that wouldn't do for the Marshal Service.

After a can of chicken noodle soup, he checked his e-mail. Another message from Kimberly, Robert's wife, was in his inbox. Another round of pictures of their girls. He wrote back with the usual pithy comments.

Doing well. Be back to Virginia soon. Hard to say when, but please tell everyone to stop worrying.

Everyone included the community of fellow marshals and their families. Minus Robert.

He'd taken part of Virginia with him anyway. His U.S. Marshal badge sat on his desk next to his computer along with a photo of Robert right after he'd received the commendation for his work uncovering white supremacist groups on the eastern seaboard. Right next to the Cuban cigar he'd given Jack that very night. Fortunately,

Jack didn't smoke, or he might not still have it.

He couldn't have known then that night would be the last time they'd celebrate any-thing together. Staring, Jack noticed with a shock that the Cuban cigar was gone from its placement near the photo. That didn't make sense, since it had sat next to the photo of Robert since he'd moved in, one of the few things he'd made sure to unpack.

He searched the room as a sinking feeling spread when he recalled that Lexi had sat at his computer the previous day. He'd left her alone for a few minutes, and it was then that she must have pocketed it.

But why would the kid steal, of all things, a rare Cuban cigar? It didn't matter why, the whole thing smacked of rebellion and unacceptable behavior. *In his own home.* He'd been right about that kid all along.

Pent up frustration bubbled over, and he fought the instinct to put his fist through the wall. *Calm down.* He could stomp over there right now, and interrupt their family dinner. The grandma would glare at him over her sumptuous fried chicken as he accused her granddaughter of being a thief.

What would Maggie do? Would she believe him or stand up for her daughter? And would she have any idea why the kid had done it?

Not that it mattered.

He had no idea why kids did half of the things they did. He couldn't go over there now; he was too upset to be rational. He'd wait until tomorrow. Either way, his favorite neighbor was about to get some lousy news because her daughter was a thief.

Chapter 5

Jack jerked awake. He'd fallen asleep staring at the bottle of sleeping pills. It sat, unopened, near his digital alarm clock.

Another night without assistance. So what if he'd tossed and turned for hours. Somewhere in there, he'd actually slept, and at least it was something. He showered and shaved, taking time to note the bags that were starting to accumulate under his eyes.

I wonder how long a man can go without sleep.

A few minutes later, he heard Maggie's SUV make its valiant efforts to start. He glimpsed outside to see Lexi run to the car and hop in the passenger seat. He'd already made up his mind to speak to Maggie about the cigar first, unable to trust that he could keep his temper in check with the kid.

That's what he got for allowing himself to be taken in by Maggie—the kid, stealing out of his home. All things considered, it was a much better idea to keep to himself, but for now he just wanted to get the cigar back.

He'd already decided he wouldn't press charges, and Calhoun would have talked him out of it anyway. But one thing was for sure: the kid would never step foot inside his house again.

A few minutes later Maggie returned, and he slowed his breathing as he strode outside to meet her.

"Hey. I need to talk to you," Jack said.

Maggie met his gaze. "Sure, what's up?"

"Can we go inside?"

The seriousness of the subject warranted privacy, and he had no idea how Maggie would react to the bad news. If there would be yelling, best to contain it indoors. In this arena, he had tons of experience.

"Of course." She moved to her front door and unlocked it.

Maggie's home was the same size and floor plan of his, but the similarities ended there. This house was a home—from the warm hues of the beige walls to the vanilla scented candles on the kitchen windowsill. Even the beige leather couch in the great room appeared to be worn in all the right places.

He took a breath. "I'm just going to say it. Something is missing from my home. From my desk, actually, and Lexi was the last person there."

"Missing?" Maggie hovered near the kitchen table where she'd placed her purse.

"Missing—as in taken from my home. Gone."

"But why do you think Lexi took it?"

He sucked in a breath. He'd been down this river called Denial with other parents, and he should have anticipated winding up there with Maggie, too.

"It was at the computer desk when she came over."

"Are you sure? Couldn't you have misplaced it somewhere?" Maggie's eyes narrowed.

"I'm sure." He'd looked at that cigar almost every night. It was all he had left of his former partner.

"I hoped you were different." Maggie's green eyes filled with fire—a forest fire.

"Different? What do you mean?" Was this where she told him that she'd expected him to perform a miracle on her troubled teen?

"That you wouldn't assume every kid is out to make trouble. Lexi's been through a tough time, but she wouldn't steal from you. Not when you invited her into your home."

Well, he hadn't invited her as much as her mother had, but that was beside the point. He'd allowed her to use his computer, and this was how he'd been repaid. No point other than to chalk this one up to experience.

Another reason to mistrust kids, as if he needed another one. "This is a matter of logic. We don't need a full-blown investigation."

"Of course not. Why should you be inconvenienced?" Maggie folded her arms across her chest.

"All I know is the cigar is missing, Lexi was there, and I want it back." Tension hovered between them, thick as early-morning fog.

The color drained from Maggie's face. She pulled out a kitchen chair and sat down with a slump. "A cigar?"

"I know it's weird that she took it, but maybe it was just a childish prank. Anyway, the cigar belonged to my partner back in Virginia. I don't smoke and it has sentimental value."

And what would a kid want with a cigar? Obviously, the whole thing had been a challenge. She'd taken it from him, perhaps as a way to repay him for mistaking her for a burglar. For staring at her mother too long. God only knew why.

"If she took it, will you press charges?" Now Maggie's lower lip quivered, and it hit him worse than a kick in the gut.

Something had changed, and now she believed him. He wished he had any idea of why. Just the thought he'd pressed charges on something like this…what must she think of him?

"I won't. I just want the cigar back."

"I'll talk to her when she gets home, and, if she took it, she will not only return it, but I'll make sure she's punished for this."

"I appreciate it. And, Maggie, kids do things for reasons you and I can't even begin to imagine." He'd learned that tough lesson, and had the scars to show for it.

"There's no excuse for this if she did it. I

don't know what's happening with my daughter anymore. But I will get to the bottom of it. I promise you."

Her eyes glistened with unshed tears, but it was better for her to know the truth now since it would get worse from here on out.

He'd seen it before.

Soon Maggie would realize that she no longer had any control over her daughter.

<hr>

AFTER JACK WALKED out the front door, Maggie worked up the nerve to glance at herself in the mirror. Her hair stuck up on one side, lying flat on the other, and one eye had a black smudge from the mascara she'd failed to completely remove last night. Jack had seen her. Like this. Vera would kill her for even leaving the house in this condition.

But her looks were the least of her problems. A nagging suspicion told her that against all reason, Lexi had taken that cigar because when Jack mentioned the missing item the truth had slammed into Maggie. Still, she didn't want to believe it. There wouldn't be any point in explaining it to Jack. He wouldn't understand. No one could. She had a difficult time under-standing it herself.

When they'd moved back to California, she'd been a zombie, packing boxes without any focus. It hadn't been possible or the right time to throw anything away, and so Matt's clothes had been packed along with his books, tools, and every memento he'd ever owned from the time of their marriage.

The Teacher of the Year Award he'd been awarded in his seventh year of teaching, the Best Coach Award for the athletic association in which Lexi had played, the prized Cuban cigar given to him by Richard on the day of Lexi's birth.

Every one of Matt's items, other than his clothes, had been misplaced in the move, and since then Lexi had tried to replace as many as possible.

Maggie played along, purchasing a Father of the Year mug similar to the one he'd drank coffee out of every morning, a flannel shirt similar to his favorite one, while she continued to search for the boxes with no luck.

And now Lexi had stepped it all up a notch, humiliating them both by stealing from their neighbor. A police officer. Maggie considered that her daughter could be that manipulative. She'd probably noticed Maggie's awkward attempts to find her a mentor and put a plug in it. Jack Butler would want to have nothing to do with either one of them again, and she couldn't very well blame him.

She'd always given Lexi a modicum of privacy in her own bedroom, but perhaps that had been a mistake. Now she marched into Lexi's room because she needed answers. Answers Lexi was not going to volunteer.

Reaching under Lexi's bed, she found a mismatched pair of socks, candy wrappers, an overdue library book, and a family of dust bunnies. But thank the Lord, no cigar. She felt between the mattress and the box spring, a place where she'd hidden her own diary as a teen, and found nothing.

If Matt were here now, he'd scold her for invading their daughter's privacy, but he'd missed out on these lovely teenage years and left Maggie holding the bag. A framed picture of Matt with Lexi's basketball team sat on the nightstand beside Lexi's bed. Maggie sat on the ground, the photo in her hands, and stared at her old life.

God, You promised You'd be with me.
Help me to remember that.

The search continued as she pulled out dresser drawers and reached into the space between them. On the second drawer, Maggie pulled out a terrycloth washrag wedged beneath, and unwrapped it. Inside its folds, she found the cigar.

Oh Lord, she hadn't wanted to find this.

Maggie backed up to Lexi's bed and slumped down on it holding the cigar.

Breathe. It'll be OK.

But what if this was just the beginning. Lexi was becoming a daughter she hardly recognized. The only thing Maggie had ever wanted was to be a good mother, and now she had failed at this, too.

She'd already failed at being a wife. Matt had made that clear enough. They'd been married too young and hadn't truly chosen each other. More like their youthful indiscretion had chosen them. Still she'd loved her husband even if he didn't want to attend church with them. Even if maybe they'd never been right for each other. She did love him. She listened when her pastor said that she could win him over with her obedience to God and love for Him.

Now Matt had left her alone to raise their daughter, and she would do that with the help of the Lord. Even if it killed her.

Hours later Maggie sat at the kitchen table, the cigar in the center, when Lexi opened the front door with her new key.

Lexi walked to the table, dropped her backpack, stared at the table, and then glared at Maggie. "Were you snooping in my room?"

"That's what you have to say for yourself?" Maggie swallowed.

She hadn't known what to expect, but she had hoped Lexi would apologize, not change the subject and find fault with Maggie.

"How did you find that?" Lexi whispered.

"The officer came over today. Did you think he wouldn't notice the cigar was missing? Did you stop and think for one second that maybe the cigar meant something to him, too?"

She stood. Did her daughter ever think about anyone but herself?

"No." Lexi sat at the table, head bent down.

"What were you thinking? Stealing?" Maggie broke the silence. "A cigar?"

Silence from Lexi. Now she stared off into the distance as though she saw something she had every intention of throttling.

"I don't even know what to say to you right now." Maggie covered her eyes.

"I knew you would overreact. So typical." Lexi rolled her eyes.

"You call *this* overreacting? I want you to tell me right now why you did this."

"You know why."

"We've talked about this. Your dad's things are not going to replace him, and you can't keep thinking that they will. And you could have asked me to buy the cigar."

"Like you would have. It's a cigar. You probably thought I wanted to smoke it."

"Sooner or later, we'll find dad's boxes." They had to be somewhere in the garage. Her throat threatened to close up on her, and she tried to take a breath.

"What do you care? You've forgotten all about him. You're glad he's gone! You guys used to fight all the time. Now it's over."

Lexi held her finger tips to her eyelids as if she could shove the tears back inside.

Maggie's breath hitched. No matter how

angry she was, her daughter was in terrible pain. "Oh, honey. It's OK to cry. I miss him, too."

"No you don't. Am I going to jail?" Lexi whispered.

Maggie pressed her hand to her forehead, a massive stress headache developing.

"He just wants the cigar back. But I'm the one you really have to worry about. I know why you did this, but it's still not OK. You're grounded for a month. And you'll have to do something for the officer during that time, like, I don't know, mow his lawn."

"Mow his lawn? I don't even know how to do that." Lexi sniffed.

"You'll learn. I'm sure he'll teach you how. Or I will as soon as I figure it out myself. And of course, you'll return the cigar."

Lexi wouldn't meet her eyes. "Will you go with me?"

"I will. I want to see you apologize to him in person."

Although there was every chance he'd never want to see either of their faces again, Lexi had to try to make amends.

"JACK, IT'S ME."

He hadn't spoken to her in months, but Kimberly Craig's voice over the phone still made him break out in a cold sweat.

"Is everything all right?"

She only served to remind him that he should be at home in Virginia. Too much time had already passed, and he cursed the fact that he was still too weak to return. He expected Kim's e-mails, but she'd never called him here before.

"I should be asking you that. When are you coming back?"

"I don't know when I'll be back." He paced the floor, running a hand through his hair.

"Help me understand. The department cleared you. You've been exonerated. What are you waiting for? Robert wouldn't want this," Kim said.

But he couldn't be convinced of that. The one thing he did know was that Robert would want to be with his family. But nothing could fix that now.

"Running away won't solve anything," Kim continued.

She didn't have to tell him that—he lived

with the nightmares that had followed him here.

"How are the girls?" Jack changed the subject.

Kim loved talking about Alison and Amber as much as Robert had. For the next few minutes, he heard about Girl Scout meetings, swim meets, and piano lessons. While he thought he'd been updated with Kim's regular e-mails, their activities made his head spin. And Robert was missing all of it.

"What about your therapy? Have you found anyone there?" Kimberly asked.

She'd been a great believer in it, even forcing Robert to take marital counseling classes though no one who knew them thought they were needed. Kim and Robert were a match made in heaven.

Therapy hadn't worked for him if Dr. Logan had been any indication. He had no interest in rehashing the past and working through his feelings, all that crazy, touchy-feely kind of talk. He'd get through this on his own, as he'd always done before.

"No. Working on it, though."

"Working on it? How can you move forward if you—?"

Jack's doorbell rang.

End of round one. Kimberly two, Jack zero.

"I've got to go, Kim. I think it's my neighbor at the door. She's got something I need."

"She's? Got something you need?" Kimberly laughed into the phone.

"No, Kim. It's not like that. I've got to go. Talk to you later."

"I'm not going to drop this, you know." Kimberly said before they ended their conversation, and somehow he didn't doubt it.

Both Maggie and Lexi stood behind his door, the cigar in Lexi's hand. "Here's your cigar, Mr. Butler. I'm sorry. Thanks for not arresting me."'

For a second, he was almost sorry for the little thief as he took the cigar from her shaking hand.

"No problem. Every thief gets one freebie from me. But only one."

"Lexi is grounded for a month, and she'll be happy to mow your lawn during that time," Maggie said.

"I don't have a lawn mower. I planned on hiring a service," Jack said.

"Even better. This will save you money.

And we have a lawn mower, except neither one of us knows how to use it." Maggie's lower lip trembled.

Heck, no, she was about to cry.

Please, not this.

"We'll let you get back to…whatever you were doing," Maggie said, and she and Lexi turned toward their home.

He shut the door and went to the desk where he placed the cigar in front of Robert's photo. Right where it belonged.

Too bad both Maggie and Lexi appeared ashamed when only one of them should be. Then again, Maggie had defended her daughter blindly and now had to face facts. It had to hurt.

A few minutes later, Maggie was back at his door again.

"I feel terrible. I didn't believe you. I hope you'll forgive me, too. Sometimes I can be a little blind when it comes to Lexi."

"You don't need my forgiveness. I'm sorry if I came on too strong. The cigar…it means a lot to me."

"I realize that," Maggie said with teary eyes.

"Are you OK?"

A stupid question. No, she wasn't OK.

Her daughter had stolen from him, after he'd done her a favor. He could only imagine her mortification.

"I should have learned how to start that lawn mower." She dissolved into tears on his doorstep.

Heart positioned squarely in his throat, he could think of nothing else to do but take her hand and pull her inside.

"I'm sorry." Maggie wiped her tears away with her thumbs.

"You don't have to apologize."

Only her difficult daughter did.

"She's not the girl she used to be. I told you that before. Well, this is just one more example. I have no idea who my own child is anymore." She bit her trembling lower lip.

Jack found a tissue and handed it to her. "You're not the only parent who's raising a troubled teen."

"Yes, but I may be the only one doing it while her grandparents judge from the sidelines."

"How's that?" This had something to do, he guessed, with the grandfather who was too busy for Lexi.

She shook her head.

"I don't want to bother you with that.

But it's only fair you know why she did this. Lexi's father passed away last year in an accident, and not to make any excuses, but Lexi took the cigar because she's trying to replace her dad's things. When we moved here, there were so many boxes. We brought everything, but now I can't find the missing boxes with the things Lexi wants to remember him with, and one of them was a silly cigar. I've tried to tell her she can't replace her dad with things, but she's obviously working through it. I keep thinking it would help if we could only find the boxes. They have to be there somewhere."

"Where do you have left to look?"

He spoke again without thinking. When would he remember that none of this was any of his concern any longer? He had Robert's cigar back.

"In the garage. We stuffed it so full of boxes I can't even park my car in there. The problem is, the movers stacked the boxes so high." She rubbed her temples.

"I can help you with that." Apparently he was no longer in control of his brain around Maggie when he'd just volunteered to spend time in a dusty garage searching through someone else's boxes.

"I have no right to ask you." Maggie's lips formed a half smile despite her watery eyes.

"You didn't ask me, and I don't mind. How about this Friday?"

He had the day off and planned to spend it hiking since the weather had turned into spring overnight, but he couldn't do that all day.

"You're very kind. I was right about you. I honestly wouldn't blame you if you wanted nothing to do with either one of us again."

And if it were anyone else but Maggie, he might have to agree.

SO HE HADN'T PITIED her and told her how sorry he was, like everyone else did when they heard the horrible news about Matt. Maggie wondered about that. Then, again, he was a police officer and had probably heard much worse. And maybe he realized that offering sad platitudes about the injustice of the world did nothing to ease a person's pain. In fact, if anything, it brought it all back up again, front and center.

At least today maybe the boxes would be

found, and they'd move forward to the next chapter in their lives. But even though the items in the missing boxes were Lexi's current fixation, Maggie couldn't help but think that there would be another issue around the corner. Mementos would only be a temporary solution. Lexi needed to turn to God to heal the hurt, but Maggie couldn't force her. She'd have to get there on her own.

Still, it had to get done even if Maggie hadn't been able to face the garage in months. Fear of spiders kept her away, and regret. One of these boxes might just send her back into the darkness again, and she couldn't afford another few months of fading away into the comfort of sleep.

On Friday, Jack arrived in the late morning wearing jeans and a faded U.S. Marshal t-shirt. Maggie tried not to notice how to shirt strained against the hard planes of his chest, and she briefly imagined what he might look like with his shirt off. *Stop it.* Why couldn't her neighbor be homely?

He frowned as he surveyed the mess of boxes.

"Hey, you weren't kidding."

"I meant it when I said we brought everything."

He got to work immediately, pulling the ladder near the row of boxes that were stacked seven-feet high and three-boxes deep.

"We need a plan. How do you want to do this?" he asked.

For the next few hours they worked together, Jack bringing down boxes that had been out of her reach for months. She'd look in them, make a judgment call, and he'd return them back to their original place.

The plastic boxes were easy to work with but when it came to the cardboard boxes Maggie held her breath. Spiders loved cardboard, and for that reason, she'd worn gloves in addition to a long sleeved cotton shirt.

Inside a cardboard box marked "Lexi," Maggie found a treasure of early art work.

A drawing Lexi made in first grade of her dad fishing, her childish scrawl ‚Mah dadi luv to fsh‘ a reminder of the precious little girl who was still in there somewhere.

Maggie set the drawing aside. Lexi would want this, and it might bring some comfort. Stiffly, she brushed aside a cobweb with her gloved hand.

And there around the lid of the box, the maker of the webs crawled out. Maggie dropped the drawing and jumped back almost as fast as the spider did. It made no sense, but suddenly she could feel the spider, or maybe its twin, crawling around in her hair.

"Yeow."

She danced around and swatted at her hair until she remembered she wasn't alone in the garage, and probably looked like a lunatic. But still she couldn't help it as she continued to whip her hair around in hopes the spider would release its hold on her.

"Is it in my hair? Because I feel like it's in my hair." Why hadn't she thought to wear a hat as well?

In between jiggles and head whips, Jack climbed down the ladder and moved toward her. She forced herself to still as he approached. He searched through her hair, one hand touching it lightly and the other holding her chin still.

"Sorry. No spider." He removed his hands, stood back, and stared in her eyes.

"Good."

She relaxed for a moment and then her stomach did a flip while her heart raced for no apparent reason other than the fact that Jack continued to gaze in her eyes.

She fixated on the blue irises. They probably only seemed intense because they contrasted against his brown hair. Neither one of them said a word.

"Hey, I'm home. What are you doing?"

Lexi dropped her backpack with a thud in the driveway of the open garage.

"We're looking for the missing boxes."

Maggie's face flushed as though she'd been caught doing something wrong, though last time she checked, staring at a good-looking man was not a sin.

"I want to help," Lexi said, moving toward an open box.

"Look what I found." Maggie handed the drawing to Lexi. "Thought you might want this."

Lexi's gaze lingered, and Maggie's heart ached at the darkness that passed over her daughter's face. The past would only hurt her more, and Maggie wondered what they were doing in here, trying to unearth it.

Chapter 6

Another few seconds and Jack would have had to apologize to Lexi, and not the other way around.

For kissing her mother.

First, Maggie had dressed like a bee-keeper, wearing gloves and a long sleeved shirt to sort through boxes. Seemed like overkill. But she'd really had his attention with the spider dance. The woman appeared to be deathly afraid of spiders, and she'd tossed that wavy mane of hair around like a white flag.

He'd tried to help but didn't expect her hair to feel like spun silk in his hands. Or to enter a staring contest, but he'd been taken in by those eyes. His hand had touched that porcelain skin, and unable to break away, he'd stood and stared like a fool until Lexi's voice broke the trance.

The hours continued to pass with only occasional breaks for the iced tea Maggie offered, and before either of them realized it, dusk had arrived. And according to every box that he offered to Maggie for perusal, they hadn't found any of the missing items.

"I owe you dinner for all this work you've done," Maggie said.

He remembered the lasagna, and hungry though he was, he couldn't handle more of Maggie's cooking.

"You don't need to go to any trouble for me."

Behind Maggie, Lexi eyed him, a smirk on her face. Did she really think he would criticize her mother's cooking and hurt Maggie's feelings?

"It's no trouble." Maggie smiled.

"I can grill," Jack offered.

Today had been a warm spring day, and summer cookouts seemed just around the bend. And even though his mind told him he should get home and prepare to fight sleep again, his body kept him tethered there.

"You don't have to do that." Maggie shook her head.

"I really don't mind," he said.

"Well, I think I have some steaks," Maggie said.

"I want hotdogs," Lexi said.

He followed them inside through the house to the outside patio filled with green potted plants hanging from hooks. A placard read:

One is nearer to God's heart in the garden than anywhere else on earth.

Maybe Maggie couldn't cook a lick, but she did have a green thumb.

"I'll go get the steaks and hotdogs," Maggie said, walking back into the house.

The grill sat in the corner, a dusty and forgotten beast.

His chest constricted as he thought of Kimberly and wondered if she'd ever learned to start the lawn mower or light the grill. He should find out. If he'd had the guts to stick around he would have been the one to take care of those things in Robert's place.

Lexi handed him some matches and directed him to the lighter fluid. She continued to glare as though he might steal the family silver.

"What are you doing?"

"I'm preparing the grill. What does it look like?" He poured some coals out of the bag.

"Why don't you just tell my mother that you hate her cooking? We both know it's true." Lexi crossed her arms.

"I didn't say that."

"You didn't have to. Why are you really here?"

"I'm helping your mother look for the missing boxes of your dad's things."

"She told you about my dad?" Her eyes widened.

"That's what this is all about—your mother, trying to make it better for you."

Lexi was about to say much more, of that he was certain, but Maggie walked outside carrying a plate of meat and wearing a floral sundress that showed off the best pair of legs he'd ever seen. He averted his eyes before the kid could notice. Too late.

"What are you *wearing*?" Lexi asked, her voice dripping with hostility.

"I found this in one of the boxes. I can't believe it still fits me."

"I can't believe you're wearing it."

"Lexi, you're being rude," Maggie warned.

Jack tightened his jaw harder with each of Lexi's words, but he kept quiet. Not his problem, but he wondered if Maggie's husband had allowed the kid to talk to her that way. He assembled the coals and poured on the lighter fluid.

"Fine. I'm sorry, but it's just that…"

Lexi glanced from him to Maggie and then back again. She groaned, threw up her hands in the air and stomped back inside the house.

Jack tossed a match on the charcoals and stepped back from the growing heat of the flames. He couldn't help it when his gaze followed Maggie as she sighed and walked to the edge of the deck where she stared into the forest of trees behind them.

"These teenage years are going to be one big carnival ride. I can tell."

"Hopefully, you like roller coasters." He tried to keep his tone light, teasing. The effort exhausted him.

"I don't. They make me sick."

The pain in those green eyes nearly undid him.

"This might be my fault. She knows you told me about her father and the boxes."

"If anyone misspoke, it would be me. Maybe I shouldn't have said anything, but I'm grateful you helped me look."

"We didn't get through everything yet."

"Sometimes I wonder if I should bother. Finding those boxes won't bring Matt back, and Lexi will realize that when we find them. Then what?"

"The next step. Facing reality. But the truth is having tangible memories does help."

He spoke of himself. Now he finally understood his ridiculous attachment to Robert's cigar. The surly teen had inadvertently taught him something about himself.

"You're probably right. I apologize again for my daughter's rudeness."

"If it helps, she's wrong. That dress looks great on you."

Maggie crossed her arms and studied the floor. Great. He'd made her uncomfortable.

"From Lexi's reaction, you would have thought I'd come out here in a swimsuit." She shook her head.

Jack swallowed at the image that formed in his mind and instead pictured bunnies and puppies.

"She doesn't care for anyone paying you attention. That sounds pretty normal right now."

"I won't be able to date until Lexi is eighteen and out of the house. The funny thing is my boss, Vera, has been bugging me to get a life and start dating."

"Sounds like she wants you to be happy." He covered the grill and stepped away from it.

"I don't think I remember *how* to date."

"Would you like a refresher course?"

What are you doing, Jack?

"I think I remember this part. Are you flirting with me?" She smiled.

"If you have to ask, I must be doing it wrong."

She covered her face with her hands and laughed. "I'm such a prize."

Yes, you are. Jack managed to keep his thoughts to himself and only laughed along with Maggie.

"I'm sorry, too, Jack."

"For what?"

"Are you kidding me? For the way I behaved when you told me about the cigar. I jumped to conclusions and accused you of being unfair."

"But you brought me back the cigar. It took a lot of courage to admit that you were wrong."

She could have kept the cigar, and no one would have been the wiser.

"As a Christian, I'm compelled to do the right thing. Now to convince my daughter to feel the same way."

"All teens rebel."

"You haven't met my Bible study partner's daughter. She's sixteen and collects food for the homeless and leads a youth Bible study. Not all teens rebel."

"The ones I've seen do."

He didn't want to go there right now. In this quiet twilight air, with Maggie's soft voice and only the sound of a light wind brushing through the trees, he could fool himself into thinking that he might avoid the nightmares tonight.

"I blame myself. Lexi wasn't raised in the church from the time she was a small child like some of the other kids. Matt and I used to argue about whether we should take her to Sunday school. Matt was a believer, but thought his parents had pushed religion down his throat, and he rebelled because of that."

"My grandfather used to take me to church, but he was the only one who ever did."

James Butler had been the only member of his family to tell Jack he'd never give up on him. Even when he'd been a hellion of the first caliber. Talk about rebellion. He could have outmatched Lexi's antics with his hands tied behind his back.

"What about your parents?"

"They're both dead now," Jack said, staring into the distance.

"I'm sorry. I don't remember my dad, and my mother died right before Lexi was born. My brother lives in New Jersey, but he has his own family. He tried to help as much as he could after Matt died, but he lives too far away."

"I guess you're lucky to have your in-laws."

Maggie opened her mouth to answer when Lexi poked her head outside. "I'm starving, if anyone cares."

"It will be just a few minutes, Lex,"

Maggie said, and something shifted in her expression.

For the few minutes he'd heard Maggie unburden her heart to him, he'd been transfixed. Something about this woman made him forget all the rules he'd put in place. He didn't want any commitments, and he didn't want to care at all. But Maggie didn't make that easy.

Earlier in the garage, he'd fought every instinct in his body to just grab her and kiss her. Long and hard. Not let her go. But there was the matter of a teenage girl who barely tolerated his presence, and he was a short timer around here. Maggie needed someone stable, and Lexi needed a father figure. Hopefully the God she and Calhoun both believed in would give her and Lexi what they needed. As for him, he'd given up asking.

Jack uncovered the lid of the grill and said the only thing of which he was certain.

"The coals are ready."

SUNDAY ARRIVED. Maggie rushed through the house throwing one last load of laundry in the dryer and then slathering a piece of toast with peanut butter. The breakfast of champions.

"Lexi, last warning. If you don't get up now we'll be late to church," Maggie said.

Lexi rolled over and spoke through a blanket of hair. "I'm coming."

Maggie took one last glimpse at herself in the mirror. No silly sundress today. She blushed at her mistake. She'd found the hideous floral dress in a box and put it on to appear less attractive. She'd realized too late, when she saw the look in Jack's and Lexi's eyes that it showed off a little too much of her legs.

He'd been enough of a gentleman to look away quickly, but the entire exchange had been so embarrassing she hoped to avoid him for a few days.

Their exchange in the garage, when he'd tenderly touched her hair, had rattled her. She didn't like these somewhat foreign feelings that reminded her of being a lovesick teenager. There would never be any more of those heady and intense feelings for her. She had a teenager of her own now.

Hopping in the car, Maggie turned the

key to dead silence. No chug-a-lug attempts to start. No sound at all. Wonderful.

"Well, maybe we can miss today."

Another bill to add to the growing list. She'd expected to need a newer car soon enough, and it looked as if the day might have just arrived.

"I don't want to miss today," Lexi said.

Maggie blinked. Lexi normally railed against church, and for a moment, Maggie wondered what had gotten into her daughter, but she wasn't about to complain.

"Maybe I can call someone to give us a ride." Maggie thought of Vera first. She'd been trying to get her to come to church anyway, and now she had the perfect excuse.

Vera answered on the fourth ring, her voice groggy. "Who is this?"

"I'm sorry I woke you up. Can you give me a ride to church? The car won't start."

"I was out late dancing the night away." Vera groaned.

Maggie didn't even know of a place in the area to go dancing. That was stuff that single people did.

"Never mind. By the time you get here, it'll be too late anyway."

"Sorry," Vera said.

Jack had noticed them sitting in the car and nodded in their direction. Today he wore gray sweats and a black baseball jersey and didn't look as if he were ready to go anywhere but back to bed. He picked up the newspaper from his lawn.

"What about him?" Lexi jutted her chin in Jack's direction.

"Jack?" Maggie worried a nail between her teeth.

Still outside, he perused the paper, a coffee mug in his other hand.

"He's already here," Lexi said.

"You're right. I'll ask."

Not that she wanted to ask. He'd already done too much for her, and they'd done little in return but cause him difficulty. Well, Lexi had done little in return.

"Hey." He looked up as she approached.

"Good morning. I hate to ask, but somehow the heavens have aligned so that my daughter actually wants to go to church today. Could we possibly get a ride?"

"I knew it was about to give up on you." He glanced in the direction of her car.

Maggie shrugged. "I put too much faith in it."

He nodded. "I'll be right back."

Maggie waved at Lexi. She expected Jack to return with his keys, but a few minutes later, he emerged wearing black slacks and a tan button-up shirt. When she stared, he looked down at his choice of clothing.

"Is this OK? I haven't been to church in years."

"You look"—devastatingly handsome came to mind—"fine."

Maggie's heart skipped a beat, and she pasted a smile on her face.

She'd spent a decade trying to get Matt to join them at church with spotty success, and now Jack had assumed he'd been invited. She wasn't about to correct him.

Jack followed her directions to Shadow Mountain Bible Church, and when he pulled into the parking lot, she didn't blame him when he stared at the building.

"This is a church?"

A former vacation home of the Serrano family, the building had been donated to the church. It had floor to ceiling windows, a pain to clean, most in the congregation complained, but Pastor Wooten said it served to remind them that people in glass houses shouldn't throw stones. It stood on a bluff overlooking the ridge.

They filed in, arriving in the middle of worship, and Lexi found her place with the young teens in their separate row.

That left Maggie and Jack alone in a row side by side. She was aware that she drew looks from some in the congregation who had never seen her attend with anyone other than Lexi.

But once she settled into her seat and Pastor Wooten continued to lead the band in worship songs, Maggie found herself lost in the worship music.

SHADOW MOUNTAIN WAS unlike any other church he'd ever attended. In the days when he'd spent southern summers in Alabama with his grandfather, every Sunday meant church and a tie. He'd listen to a sermon from a pastor who made him feel guilty about how he spent the rest of the week—not to mention the rest of the year.

This pastor led the band with his twelve string guitar. The man looked to be about Jack's age, wore a shark tooth around his neck, and looked as if he were missing his surfboard. Jack wondered if maybe he was the pastor's son run amuck for the day.

And then there was Maggie's voice. As he stood next to her, it lifted above the rest of the congregation and sounded like an angel had appeared at his side.

Pastor Wooten grasped his attention with the sermon as he jumped about on stage describing his experience bungee jumping and made it an analogy to being ‚all in‘ for Christ. Church had definitely changed in the past twenty years, even though he'd had no real idea what to expect. Still, teens wore half ripped jeans and pink hair, and no one even seemed upset about it.

As they walked outside, they ran into Sheriff Calhoun.

"Good to see you, Jack. I knew it would take a woman to get you here." He slapped Jack's back.

Maggie flushed. "You know each other?"

"Calhoun is my boss," Jack said.

"I thought you were retired," Maggie said as she glanced at Calhoun.

"Not yet. Soon though." His voice boomed above the crowd of voices.

"Jack is my neighbor, and he was kind

enough to bring us this morning when my car wouldn't start," Maggie said.

"What's wrong with it?" Calhoun asked.

"It's old," Maggie said.

Calhoun laughed and patted her back. "I'll send my mechanic to take a look. He's someone you can trust."

"I can't afford much right now." Maggie stared intently over Calhoun's shoulder.

Jack followed Maggie's gaze. She fixated on Lexi, standing with a shaggy haired boy he recognized all too well. Anton Whitman was the son of Tim Whitman and on a first name basis with law enforcement.

Anton had become quite fond of vandalizing the fence downtown with his spray painted "art." So far, he'd accumulated thousands of dollars of personal property damage, which his father had paid. Naturally, he had to keep up appearances, but in all likelihood, Jack would bet Tim made Anton pay dearly for his indiscretions behind closed doors.

Normally Jack didn't have much sympathy for teens like Anton, but having personally become acquainted with his father had given him a new found compassion for the kid.

For Maggie's sake, he kept one eye trained on Anton as both kids approached.

"Mom, can we give Anton a ride home?" Lexi walked up to Maggie.

"That depends." She looked at Jack, a question in her eyes. "Is that OK?"

"It's fine." He glanced at Anton, who wouldn't meet his eyes. Typical. Out of his uniform or in it, he was a non-person to some kids.

Calhoun slapped Anton on the back. "Good to see you here, son."

He didn't ask after the family, which made Jack wonder how Anton had made it here this morning. It was a long hike from his palatial home to town, and he didn't know too many kids who would do it to sit through a sermon, bungee-jumping pastor or not. Unless. Yeah, it had to be Lexi.

They said their good-byes and proceeded to his truck. He unlocked the doors and glanced at Maggie, who turned to him. "You're sure this is OK?"

Although it didn't bother him, he couldn't say the same about Maggie. She wore a similar expression to the one she had when she'd wrung her hands and begged him to agree to speak to Lexi.

"It's fine."

He opened the passenger door for Maggie and waited for her to climb in. The truck wasn't exactly equipped for petite women like her, and he had to resist the urge to help her. Better to keep his hands to himself.

"You'll have to tell Mr. Butler how to get there, Anton," Maggie said once they were all seated in his truck.

"I know the way," Jack said.

"Oh."

Maggie sounded as though she'd connected the dots, a good thing because he wouldn't lie for Anton. On the other hand, neither did he need to ruin everything for the kid who, after all, had made it to church. Surely, that had to be progress for him. *Take it easy, Butler.*

Jack drove them slightly out of town to the gated community he'd nicknamed la-la land for street names like La Mar, La Honda, and La Pala. This was where the privileged of Harte's Peak lived.

As they entered Sierra Estates, Lexi made a tiny gasp. "This is where my grandma and grandpa live."

Anton directed him to drop him off at

the curb. No surprise. He leaped out of the truck without a backward glance or so much as a thank you.

"Mom, can we stop and visit Grandma and Grandpa?"

He glanced at Lexi through the rearview mirror as she jumped up and down on the seat. He did a double take because she suddenly sounded like she was seven.

"This isn't a good time. I'm sure Mr. Butler has things to do, and he's our ride," Maggie said.

"Sorry."

While all he had ahead of him tonight was a swing shift, neither did he want to visit anyone's grandparents. Besides, he got the distinct impression Maggie didn't want to stop by either, with or without him.

Surprisingly, the kid seemed to accept the news without complaint, sighing only once. Probably some kind of record.

Jack pulled into his driveway.

Lexi grabbed the keys, jumped out of the truck, and ran to her house.

Maggie stayed back. "I'd like to talk to you about Anton sometime, and exactly how you know him."

Glancing toward her house, he nodded. "Sure."

He'd meant to compliment her voice—the sound of an angel—but she was gone like the wind before he had a chance. She belonged in the choir or someplace where others could appreciate that distinctive, almost pleading sound. Not that he was any expert, but he did have a pair of ears, which hadn't failed him yet.

Today's sermon from the pastor might have been encouraging if they could have applied to him, but some things were beyond forgiveness. Surely, God wanted everyone to stop being a bunch of whiners, anyway. He didn't believe in begging God for help any more than he believed in therapy. Weaker people needed God. Not him. The thing to do was pull yourself up by your own sheer willpower.

Sooner or later he'd do it, too, with the same single-minded determination that got him through military school and into the Marines. From the Marines he'd found a place in the Marshal Service, a place he belonged. No whining. He never had before, and he wasn't about to start now.

On the other hand, James Butler was probably smiling today seeing him in a church pew again. The man had never missed a Sunday until the day he died.

If not for his grandfather, his life would have turned out quite differently. He might still be living with his mother, might have even been the one to find her dead from the drug overdose. But he'd been spared all that when Child Protective Services had intervened and placed him with his grandfather, the one man who'd sworn he'd never give up on him.

He couldn't give up on himself, either, but what he'd done so far wasn't working. Maybe it was time to try a new tactic. Dr. Logan had said that the pills were only a temporary measure, but he didn't believe it. Neither was it likely that his colleagues had accepted the excuse that he'd taken a personal leave of absence to take care of a family issue. He wondered what Kim had told them, if anything.

They probably thought he was nuts, loco, off the deep end. And every moment he spent away was another moment he failed to convince them otherwise. Still, if he returned now, as Kimberly thought he should, he couldn't face any of them.

Not when he could barely look at his own reflection in the mirror.

Chapter 7

Jack sat in the patrol car at the intersection of Main and Second Street.

Ryan sat beside him in the driver's seat. "If something doesn't happen in this town soon, I might just have to poke my own eye out for the excitement."

So far, drivers had obeyed every stop sign, every stoplight of the three in town, and the speed limit. Of course, everyone managed to do so when they saw the cruiser in traffic.

Jack fought to keep his eyes open, because he'd worked the swing shift the night before. Now he worked the morning shift at Lonnie Smith's request. Might as well work because he still wasn't having much luck with sleep.

"What do you have against peace and quiet?" Jack asked.

"I've now had enough of it to last me a lifetime." Ryan, an ex-professional competitive skier sidelined by a career-ending injury, apparently hadn't adjusted to the slower pace in Harte's Peak.

"Not what you had in mind growing up playing cops and robbers?"Jack asked.

"Yesterday I spent the day on the side of the highway catching speeders. Ben Bailey whipped out a fake ID. A bad one, with the picture scotched-taped on and barely in place. It's the most excitement I've had in weeks." He sighed.

"Catch Vera again?" Jack lifted one eyebrow.

The owner of The Bean, Maggie's boss, was notorious for whipping through town in her BMW as though the speed limits somehow didn't apply to her. Worse, she seemed to think her good looks entitled her to talk her way out of tickets. Not with him, though Ryan was an easy target.

"Nah. That would have made my day." Ryan grinned.

Ryan definitely had a crush on Vera. "Why don't you just ask her out?"

"I do, about once a month."

"Well, don't give up. Sooner or later she'll give in," Jack said with a laugh.

"What about you? Have you asked out your neighbor yet?" Ryan wiggled his eyebrows.

"Me? What makes you think I would ask her out?"

He didn't like it when Ryan pretended to know what he thought. Not everyone had Ryan's one track mind about women.

"Why wouldn't you?" Ryan fiddled with the visor while they sat at a long stoplight.

"One reason. The kid." The teenager he'd been asked to mentor. What a joke.

"Yeah. I can't blame you. I once dated a woman with a kid and let me tell you, if the kid doesn't like you, there's no chance."

He hadn't told Ryan about the cigar because the fact that he'd been fooled by another teenager was nothing short of humiliating. As far as he was concerned, the theft would remain between the mother, daughter, and the one who'd been duped.

"Anyway, I won't be here much longer." Maybe if he'd start saying it out loud more it would come true.

"Where are you going?" Ryan's brow

furrowed.

"Back to Virginia."

Kimberly wanted him to, and ever since her last phone call, the guilt had pressed down. Maybe he was supposed to be taking Robert's place somehow, though he never could. He'd never be half the man that Robert had been.

"When?"

That was the question of the hour. "Soon, I hope."

"Guess I can't blame you. The most excitement I get around here is the occasional paper cut."

"That's not why I'm going back."

"Why, then?"

Going back wouldn't change anything, not in any real way. He'd have to face Kimberly again, and he wasn't sure if being around her would be any different now. The last time he'd barely been able to look at her since he'd failed her as much as he'd failed Robert. And now she was a single mom. Like Maggie.

"Honestly, I'm not sure anymore. I just know that I have to. Running away doesn't solve anything."

A true friend, Ryan didn't ask any more

questions.

MAGGIE WASN'T sure whether unloading on Vera would do any good, but she couldn't stop herself. It helped that Vera was a good listener, and she stayed quiet as Maggie explained Lexi's latest antics. The cigar theft from their neighbor, a cop, and now this new friend she hadn't told Maggie anything about.

"And yesterday, I asked her for the rest of the day to tell me something, anything, about Anton, but she wouldn't. She just kept telling me he's her friend and nothing more."

"Is that all? Are you done?" Vera pushed a button on the drip machine that would start another pot of coffee.

"Isn't that enough? I've got a serious problem."

Why couldn't Vera see the danger that was imminent? Her daughter and *a boy!*

"I see that you think it's serious."

"That's because it is." Maggie stopped dipping carafes in the sudsy water and locked gazes with Vera.

"Well, I'll grant you that the cigar is a new one for me. Never thought I would hear about a kid stealing a cigar, but when I think of the reason, it makes my heart break. And honestly, Lexi is not the first girl in history to keep something from her mother."

"No, but—"

"Are you going to stand there and tell me you never kept anything from your mother?" Vera raised one perfectly shaped eyebrow.

Not unless one counted fooling around with Matt when she had no business doing so, getting pregnant, and keeping it from her mother for the first two months.

"Your silence is speaking volumes." Vera laughed.

"OK, so I kept some things from my own mother. But that's not what I wanted for my daughter." She sighed. "I was going to do it better."

"How?"

"Keep the lines of communication open, talk to her about boys, and let her know she can always come to me. It just all happened so quickly."

It seemed like such a short time ago that Lexi was still cuddly and affectionate, but now everything had changed. Matt was gone, and on Lexi's thirteenth birthday a gong had sounded somewhere in the world and turned her daughter into some kind of cactus resistant to mother's hugs.

"So how have you been different than your mother?"

She'd benefited from June Callahan's trust, deserved or not. There had never been any question that Maggie would keep and raise Lexi, and Mom offered her support in every way. And though they'd always been close, there were some things you didn't tell your mother. Some of the things a girl didn't tell her mother made her breath catch in her throat now.

"It just dawned on me that I've been a lot like my mother. Trusting, expecting the best. The truth is, when I stopped telling my mother everything, it was because I had something to hide."

"Like sneaking off with boys?"

"Exactly."

"So you shouldn't be surprised that Lexi won't tell you if she likes this boy as more than a friend. You do remember what it's like."

"I remember that there were times I wished my mother would interfere, stop me somehow. Save me from myself. It was so easy to fool her because she trusted almost too much."

"So you think you want to be a little less trusting?"

"Maybe." Maggie shook her head. "I mean, yes."

"You want to be like my Aunt Debbie." Maggie stared at Vera. "What do you mean?"

"My mother allowed me to go to Europe for my modeling career as a teenager. Then you have my Aunt Debbie. That woman should have opened her own detective agency. It all started with her husband. He cheated on her, and she found out by tailing him. As a teen, my cousin was pretty wild. My aunt used to follow her in her station wagon, and she got pretty good at it. My poor cousin never knew when my aunt would be tailing her."

"So she had to behave because she never knew when her mother might be following?"

This sounded promising. Finally, a good idea.

"Nah, she just got better at sneaking around." Vera smiled as she opened the door to their first customers.

Thoughts of Vera's enterprising aunt filled her head all morning as she filled orders for macchiato and mochas. She didn't want to spy on her own daughter, but she had to find a realistic way of knowing what was going on in that teenage mind of Lexi's. No more mistakes could be made when her in-laws watched, waiting for an opportunity for her to slip up. As the morning rush ended, Maggie pulled Vera aside.

"I need to borrow your car."

"My car? What for?" Vera's face turned pale. Her precious sporty car was like her child.

"I'm going to spy on Lexi at lunch time. It's the only way I'll know what's going on."

"When will I learn to keep my mouth shut?" Vera put a hand to her forehead.

"Your aunt was on to something. I don't know why I didn't think of it myself. I'll drive over and just sit in the car and watch them come out at lunch time."

"But—why in my car?"

"Did you forget? I walked here this morning; my car is out of commission. This all has to be undercover, like your aunt. Lexi wouldn't expect to see your car there."

"I knew I shouldn't have said anything."

She shook her head.

"Nonsense. You've been a great help. My eyes are wide open, and they'll never shut again. So, keys?" Maggie held out her hand.

"Fine, but this is a bad idea, and I want it on record that I said so."

Vera placed the keys to her BMW in Maggie's hands. "Take good care of it. And whatever you do, don't speed. Ryan issued a warning last week. He's not letting me off again."

___

MAGGIE DETERMINED within minutes that sporty cars like Vera's were great for spying on people. Her problem was that like her own mother, she'd been too trusting. Too trusting of Matt, her in-laws, Lexi. The only one she could really trust in was the Lord, and she was pretty sure He'd approve of her looking out for the one person He'd put in her care.

She sat low in the seat as she pulled alongside the curb on Main Street, where the fenced in schoolyard faced the street. From here, she had a good view of the kids as they came out of class and stood in the lunch line as it snaked outside.

Now that spring had arrived and the temperatures rose into the sixties, the kids ate their lunch outside under the large awning that covered the tables. Some kids wandered past the tables and on to the grassy knoll area as Maggie craned her neck toward the passenger side of the car.

She noticed Lexi standing alone in the lunch line, and her heart dropped. She'd hoped that by now Lexi would be part of a group of girlfriends. Instead, she looked so helpless and alone. *Lord, when will the mistakes stop adding up?*

She should have never moved back to Harte's Peak, never agreed to move out here at Paula and Richard's insistence. Being close to extended family or not, Lexi had been forced to abandon all her friends. No wonder she was having such a difficult time. Maggie shut her eyes against the pain.

No. She wouldn't go there again. God had pulled her out of that, out of the darkness and depression that had threatened to ruin everything.

When Maggie opened her eyes again, and with what looked to be an answered prayer, Lexi was no longer alone. But the problem with this new picture was that

Anton had sidled up next to her, and in a matter of seconds, the two were holding hands. Lexi and Anton looked like much more than friends.

A few of the kids stared in her direction, causing Maggie to slink down further in her seat. There was nothing wrong with watching her own kid, but she sure didn't want Lexi to see her.

She heard another car pull up beside her and turned to see Jack and Ryan in the cruiser. Jack, sitting in the passenger seat, leaned out the window and motioned for her to roll down her own.

Busted. She swallowed and obeyed his request.

"Yes?"

"Maggie, what are you doing here?" Jack's brow was furrowed in confusion. Surely, he didn't suspect her of doing anything wrong.

"Why? Is there a problem? I'm not parked illegally, am I?"

She tried to dig up some righteous indignation from where she'd left it behind, somewhere in her teen years. Stupid police, ruining her good time.

"We just got a call that someone suspicious in a vehicle was observing the kids from the street," Jack said.

"And actually, you shouldn't park here," Ryan said from the driver's side.

He probably loved this, her punishment for turning him down. She couldn't go out with Ryan when anyone with a lick of sense could see he and Vera belonged together. Not that she could go out with anyone, but especially not Ryan.

Both of them looked as if they could hardly keep a straight face. Ryan turned his face away from her, but she noticed his shoulders shaking, and Jack bit his lip as though he was trying not to smile.

Lord, please let the ground open up and swallow me whole.

The cruiser had now gathered them even more attention, and some of the students began to turn their heads and stare in their direction. If Lexi noticed her, she'd never live this down. She had to get out of here, and fast.

"I'm sorry. I'll leave now if that's OK. If you want to give me a ticket, follow me."

She didn't wait for an answer but started up the car again and pulled out into traffic praying they wouldn't follow, sirens blazing.

Soccer mom, caught loitering, evades police.

She'd probably make tomorrow's headline in the Harte's Peak Times.A check of the rearview mirror told her they were not following her. Maggie rubbed her neck and tried to ease the strain.

Back at the café, Maggie explained what had happened to Vera, leaving out as many embarrassing details as possible.

"Don't worry. You didn't do anything wrong." Vera didn't crack a smile, no doubt realizing Maggie's mortification.

"How do I know that? Somebody thought I was suspicious. And isn't there some law about loitering near a school or something?"

"Calm down, Maggie. As long as Lexi didn't see you, that's all you really had to worry about."

"You didn't see the look on Jack's face. Let alone Ryan, who looked like he would burst out laughing at any second."

"Forget about Ryan. Anyone knows you're an overzealous mom, not some kind of criminal. Take it easy."

Overzealous mom. Is that what I've become?

"And by the way, I saw Lexi with Anton, and they are definitely more than friends."

"Boyfriend or not, Lexi made one mistake. She's a good kid deep down, and you can trust her."

Spoken by a woman who didn't have children.

"Oh, sure, I can trust her. In the same way my mother could trust me? You mean in that way?"

Vera put her hand on Maggie's shoulder. "Deep breath."

But then the glass door to the café opened, and Jack strode in alone. That uniform—the gun holstered near his slim hips, the whole cop look—did nothing but good things for him, and Maggie's heart raced into overdrive.

Good friend that she was, Vera stepped forward from behind the counter, finger pointed.

"Now listen, Jack Butler. Maggie didn't do anything wrong. So if you're here to tell her so, I'd like to know what Penal Code she violated. Overprotective Mom Code 101?"

Hands thrust on her waist, Vera tossed her pale blonde hair to the side. If she wasn't Maggie's best friend, she might just have to hate her for being so beautiful.

"No violation," Jack said. "I just want to

talk to my neighbor. If that's OK with you, of course."

Vera stepped aside. "You can ask her."

"Can we have a seat, Maggie?" Jack gestured toward one of the empty tables.

Maggie let out a breath and took a seat. "Are you going to write me a ticket or lecture me?"

He took a chair across from her. "Neither. You didn't do anything wrong."

"Not unless you count being clueless."

The first real smile she'd seen on him tipped his lips.

Wow. I was right. Devastating.

"We get one silly call a day, usually from people who are bored. This is not the first time someone has called in a report that turned out to be false."

"So why are you here?"

"I feel like I should apologize." His blue eyes were warm and inviting.

"*You?* Apologize to me?"

"I left you hanging about Anton, and you must be curious. I should have taken the time to explain and not leave you to your imagination. I see you let it get the best of you."

"That's probably true."

And though she was still curious about that, Anton could have been the pastor's son and she would have still been anxious about this situation.

"So ask me whatever you want to know." He set his palms on the table.

"Really?"

"Go ahead."

"How did you know where Anton lived without asking?"

"A couple of reasons. And this is just between us. Anton's father is Attorney Tim Whitman."

"The defense attorney?" She'd just seen him on television last week, defending a young woman accused of murdering her child.

"Yes, his family lives here and so does Tim when he's not flying all over the state to defend his clients." Jack's lips were a thin straight line.

Clearly no love lost between him and Mr. Whitman.

"What does this have to do with Anton?"

"When Tim's in town we get called to the house often by the neighbors for noise complaints, domestic disturbances."

"You said there was another reason."

"Ah, well, Anton fancies himself to be quite the artist. With a spray paint bottle."

"Oh." Maggie's heart dropped.

This wouldn't have been her first choice for a boyfriend for Lexi, because her first choice was no boyfriend at all. This wasn't happening. She'd make sure of it.

"Actually, Anton's not the worst kid I've met in town. I guess that's small comfort, but it's true, and there's the fact that his home life is less than ideal."

"Has he made restitution for his art work?"

"His dad takes care of that." Jack smirked. "Mostly because he has no choice if he wants to avoid having his son work it off with community service. Most of the kids working community service hours off are pretty troubled. It wouldn't do to have his kid mixing with that crowd, I'm guessing."

"I knew this would be a roller coaster, but I didn't know this particular ride would start so soon. I am so not ready for this." She couldn't help but cradle her head in her hands.

"Yeah. I could tell." His mouth twisted back another one of those smiles.

Please don't hold back. Not on my account.

"She's too young for a boyfriend. I won't have it."

Maybe the thing to do was put her foot down and be extremely strict with Lexi since she'd never tried that approach. Lexi had always been a good kid until recently.

"I'll keep an eye out for Lexi. I promise you that."

"You've already tried to help. You talked to Lexi like I asked you to and she repaid you by—well, you know." She feared what might come next if he tried to help.

"It's not a problem."

"I wouldn't blame you if you wanted nothing to do with either one of us," Maggie said.

Jack cocked his head and his voice was soft when he spoke. "Why?"

It amazed her that he didn't realize. But then he was probably used to difficult kids, something she had no experience with before. Thanks to Lexi, she was becoming an expert.

"You really have to ask that? After the cigar?"

"I did get it back."

"But she still has to pay restitution. I'm sending Lexi over soon so you can teach her how to mow your lawn."

"It's really not necessary."

"Yes it is. I can't tell you how sorry I am that I didn't believe you right away. I've been told that I always want to see the best in people. Especially my daughter."

"There's nothing wrong with hoping for the best in people. Maybe the world needs more people like you in it, and less like me." He sounded like he meant it, and Maggie swallowed.

"You don't mean that. You're a cop, and it's your job to suspect people. I suppose somebody has to do it."

"Well, the cigar meant a lot to me."

"You and Lexi have that in common. Did a good friend give you the cigar to celebrate his baby's birth?"

"No. Nothing like that. Robert, my old partner, gave it to me when he celebrated a promotion."

"And that was a memorable occasion. Sure, it makes sense."

"I'm starting to think I was wrong about hanging on to it, though."

"Why?"

"You were right. The cigar is just a thing. But it isn't really the cigar, you know. It's the memory. When I look at that cigar, I can still see the expression on Robert's face the day he handed it to me. Kind of cocky, like he'd known the day was coming."

"Proud."

"Yeah. That was Robert."

A veil came over his eyes, and though Maggie wanted to ask so much more, something told her there were some things which would best remain unsaid.

Chapter 8

Later at the station, Jack filed a report that the suspicious person was nothing more than a parent checking on her own kid. He smiled, remembering the expression on Maggie's face, as though she'd been caught doing something wrong. The call had probably been legitimate and that of a protective teacher, but the only harm done today had been to Maggie's pride.

After he and Ryan had enjoyed a good laugh and got it out of their system, he'd had to comfort Maggie. The whole thing had really been his fault. He should have told Maggie about Anton that very day and not left her guessing. She'd probably come up with a lot worse scenarios.

Jack looked up from his paper work as the door to the station opened, and Mrs. Lenore Jones made her way inside holding a dog leash. At the end of that leash was a mangy looking dog that had seen better days.

He considered rendering assistance to Mrs. Jones, but the last time he'd tried, he'd been rewarded with a severe tongue lashing. Officially Harte's Peak's oldest citizen, according to Calhoun, Mrs. Jones seemed to think that any offers of help meant she'd be considered feeble.

"Hello, Mrs. Jones," he said, standing. The woman brought out the Boy Scout in him.

"Good afternoon, young man. I'm here about this dog and all his funny business." She handed him the leash and settled herself into the chair across from his desk.

Jack led the dog to his side of the desk nearly falling back at the strong smell of garbage.

At least the dog had the decency to look embarrassed, if that were possible. Upon closer inspection, he looked like some kind of shepherd mix.

"Funny business?"

With Mrs. Jones, one never knew. Once she'd driven to the station to report that someone had parked their car too close to a fire hydrant. Calhoun spent an hour with her, explaining that she could have just called it in. Mrs. Jones argued that there were not many places left for her to drive to anymore, since church was within walking distance of her home, and that as long as she still had her license she intended to put it to good use.

"Someone has got to take this poor dog." She raised her chin. "I can't have him digging up my prize- winning lilies anymore."

"Have you tried the Humane Society?" Jack frowned at the dog.

Maybe with a bit more meat on his bones, he might almost look—well, maybe not.

Mrs. Jones looked at him as if he were a simpleton.

"Son, they turn them into dog meat over there. I may not be able to keep him, but I sure don't want him dead. Well? So what will you do about it?"

He supposed this was what small town police work had brought him to. Now he somehow had to find a home for this creature.

"I'll make a few calls."

"See that you do. There is somebody in this town who needs a dog. Surely he's good for something." She jutted her chin in the mutt's direction.

Most prospective dog owners probably wanted one that didn't look like he'd spent the past few months living in a garbage can, but Jack promised to try.

"Thanks for bringing him in."

The mutt had parked himself near the water cooler and stared longingly at an empty box of donuts on Calhoun's desk.

Ryan walked in from the back room and stopped in his tracks when he noticed the dog.

"What is *that*?"

"Why, it's a dog. Are you blind?" Mrs. Jones asked.

"That's not a dog. That's a walking furry garbage can." Ryan frowned.

"If you clean him up, I bet he'll look like a dog again," Mrs. Jones said with a finger wag.

"That's mighty optimistic of you, Mrs.

Jones." Ryan walked to the other side of the office, holding his nose.

"It's under control," Jack said.

Surely Calhoun would take pity on the dog. Man of God and all. How could he turn this poor animal down?

"I'll be going home now." Mrs. Jones rose to leave, and both Jack and Ryan moved in her direction, but she held up a hand. "And I don't need any help."

It took Mrs. Jones several long minutes to make her way to the door, during which Jack stared alternatively at the mutt and at Ryan, who stood, body wound tight as a new guitar cord. He wanted to open that door, but he also knew better.

"What will you do with that?" Ryan frowned in the direction of the dog after Mrs. Jones left.

"I thought you loved dogs." The mutt stared at him. Jack stared back.

"I love dogs. That thing isn't a dog."

"Oh c'mon, stop exaggerating."

"We'll need to have the station fumigated now." Ryan went around the office opening windows.

"Take him home, and tomorrow Calhoun will take pity on him," Jack said.

"I can't take him home. I live in an apartment. At least you live in a house."

"I can't have a dog." He stopped short of saying that he didn't want any attachments even though it was the truth.

"Like you told me. It's just for one night."

He lived in a house with no lease, a month to month arrangement with a land-lord so desperate to fill the vacancy that she didn't mind a short timer. Because that's what Jack was around here, and no amount of pitiable dogs, elderly ladies, troubled teens, or beautiful mothers would change that.

THEY WERE GOING to have a serious talk. No more waiting patiently until Lexi wanted to confide in her. Maggie wanted to know everything—the names of Lexi's friends and their parents' names, where they lived, where they went to church, and possibly their drivers' license numbers and blood types. Secrets were dangerous, and she couldn't allow Lexi to keep them from her. How could she protect her if she didn't know what she was doing at all times?

Even so, she had no idea how to approach the subject. Matt was always best at tiptoeing the fine lines of confrontation. To Maggie, the best way was to just dive right in. Except that hadn't worked so well in the recent past.

"We need to talk." Maggie pounced the moment Lexi walked in the door after school.

"About what?" Lexi put her backpack down and turned around, her brown eyes narrowed.

"I know you have a boyfriend—"

"No, I don't!"

"Let's not do this. If you and I can't be honest with each other, we'll never make it."

Lexi pouted. "What's the point? You don't believe me anyway."

"I can see you really like Anton."

"That doesn't mean he's my boyfriend."

"Just because I told you that you couldn't have a boyfriend until you were sixteen doesn't mean that you have to lie to me now."

"I'm not lying. Ugh, I can't believe you." Lexi stomped toward her bedroom.

"Hey, don't try to make this about me!"

Lexi had inherited her father's talent at turning every argument around to make it seem as though Maggie was the one at fault.

"It's always about you. You can't let go. You can't let me live my life. You have to be in every part of my business." Lexi slammed the door to her bedroom.

Maggie was right behind her and the door almost hit her in the nose. "Lexi, open this door. I have something I need to tell you."

"Go away!"

Great, she had no idea how to do this. A teenage daughter was a phenomenon beyond her mere human abilities.

Lord, I need You now. A little guidance would be nice. It's a good thing You make house calls.

The phone rang, intruding on her silent prayer. Maggie took a breath and answered it, only to find Paula on the other line.

"How is everything? You both OK?"

The woman had some sort of honing radar when it came to Lexi. "Fine, Paula. What's up?"

Paula's voice was quiet and tentative. "I wanted to ask you if Lexi could spend the weekend with us. We don't see her often enough."

"We've been over this. I don't feel comfortable given everything that happened." How quickly Paula seemed to forget.

"Maggie, when are you going to forgive us?" Paula's voice grew harsh, tinny.

"I have forgiven you."

That much was true. She was required to forgive, and she'd done that. Reluctantly.

"In two weeks there is an art show in Sonoma, and Richard and I would love to take her. We'd make a weekend out of it; maybe take her to San Francisco, as well. You know she'd love it."

Paula had pulled at the string of guilt perpetually attached to Maggie's heart. She knew full well how much her daughter would enjoy the show, but she had more important matters to deal with at the moment. None of which she would share with Paula.

"Of course she would enjoy it, but that's not the point. I'll have to talk to you about this later. I'll call you back."

Maggie hung up, unable to deal with Paula right now. *One fight at a time, Maggie, one at a time.*

She'd given Lexi enough time to cool

down. Taking deep breaths, she calmly opened the door to Lexi's bedroom. Her daughter lay on her trundle bed, ear buds in, back facing the door.

"Ready to talk?" Maggie nudged her daughter's shoulder.

Lexi pulled the ear buds out. "Are you ready to listen?"

Well, maybe she deserved that. "Sure."

"Anton is mostly just my friend, but I think he likes me. Still, I don't like him. Not that way. Last Sunday he asked me if he could go to church with me, and I told him OK, that I'd meet him there. Because of all the kids I know, Anton needs church the most. And that's about it. Not that you'll believe me or anything."

"OK. I believe you. Just be sure that you don't keep the truth from me just because you think I won't like it."

She had a strong sense of déjà vu since she'd done the same with her own mother and failed to confess that she and Matt were dreaming about getting married and spending too much time alone together.

And then came Lexi.

Lexi stayed silent, and drew her lips into a nearly perfect pout.

"Lexi, are you OK with the Lord?" Right now, more than anything, she wanted to know that her daughter hadn't turned her back on everything she'd taught her to believe.

"You don't have to worry about that," Lexi said.

Oh, how I want to believe that.

Maggie thought about Paula's invitation so that she could demonstrate that honesty went both ways, but if she shared that with Lexi right now she'd only have to deny her one more thing. Because she still couldn't trust Paula and Richard Bradshaw with Lexi. Not yet.

Maybe a breath of fresh air would do them both some good.

"Let's go outside and figure out how to start the lawn mower."

"Oh joy," Lexi said.

The dirty mutt he'd taken to calling Chief liked tailgate rides. Jack tied his leash safely in the cab, and Chief stood in place and took in the scenery like he was a traveling dignitary. The citizens of Harte's Peak were probably all getting a good whiff of last week's trash, but at least he got a few smiles from the townsfolk as they waved at

Chief from their vehicles. And maybe somehow Chief was getting aired out. One could hope, anyway.

Tomorrow he'd take the dog back to the station and prevail on Calhoun's sense of goodness and faith in mankind. Surely, that extended to the animal species. One night with a stray dog. He could handle that, but before Chief could enter his house, he'd have to be hosed down.

He pulled into his driveway only to find Maggie on his lawn dressed in shorts and a t-shirt, bent over a lawn mower while she jerked repeatedly at the cord. Then she looked at the machine, hand on hips, and pulled at it again.

Lexi stood nearby, arms folded across her chest, the picture of teenage disinterest. That is, until she saw the back of his cab. That's when a smile began to spread from ear to ear that gave her the appearance of a much younger kid. All that teenage surliness seemed to have taken off for parts unknown as she rushed to the back of his truck.

"Mom! Look at this. Oh, the poor thing. What did you do to it?" She shifted her gaze to Jack, eyes blazing.

"What did *I* do to it?" Jack asked. "I rescued this beast. Don't blame me for the way he smells. Blame his trash gorging habits."

He untied the leash, and the dog jumped down and sat next to him as though he'd issued a command.

Maggie joined them though she almost immediately backed away, no doubt at the rancid smell. Why the smell didn't seem to affect Lexi was a mystery.

"What happened to him?" Maggie asked.

"Mrs. Jones brought him in today and wants us to find him a home. I'll bring him back tomorrow when Sheriff Calhoun is there, and I'm sure he'll figure something out."

"You're just going to give him away to some stranger?"

Lexi stared daggers at him. She was actually petting the dog, which made his opinion of her ratchet up several degrees. The kid had guts.

"Well, what do you suggest?" he asked.

"Let me wash him for you. I'll make him shine and smell so good you'll never want to give him away!"

He liked that grin on her much better than the usual scowl. Made her seem almost human.

"You would do that?"

He'd been prepared to do the honors with the hose's spray nozzle and the benefit of some distance, but soap and TLC would probably work much better.

"Yes, as long as I can skip mowing your lawn today. My mom and I were getting ready to do that, but we can't figure out how to turn it on. Anyway, I'll get your lawn all wet washing him. By the way, what's his name?"

"He doesn't have a name, so I call him Chief."

"That's a perfect name for him," Lexi said.

Great. Had he just inadvertently named a dog? It wasn't supposed to be his name, it was just temporary. A place holder. Before he could protest, Lexi had the hose, and Maggie had brought a big bucket of soapy water out of her house.

Maggie stepped back and let Lexi do the honors. The teenaged hellion tenderly let Chief guzzle water from the hose which he did as if he hadn't had a drink in weeks. Before long, the mutt was wet and sudsy, and Lexi cooed like he'd once heard a mother talk to her newborn.

"She loves dogs," Maggie said. "When we moved, one of my promises to soften the blow of leaving all her friends behind was that I'd get her a dog."

"She can have this one." Problem solved.

"No, she can't. Why are you always trying to give things away? Anyway, my landlord won't allow pets. If I'd had any sense at all, I wouldn't have made a promise that I wasn't sure I'd be able to keep."

Jack had promised Robert that he'd have his back, but that hadn't worked out quite the way he'd planned. The way he saw it, human beings were lousy at keeping promises.

"She's like a different kid," Jack said, as they watched Lexi rinse the soap off.

"This is the daughter I know, the one you've never met. Jack Butler, meet Lexi Bradshaw when she's human." Maggie turned to him and waved her hand in Lexi's direction.

It wasn't just the smile, but the way her

shoulders relaxed, and for the first time since he'd met her he heard the sound of Maggie's laughter. That girlish giggle woke something up inside of him, and he wondered what he'd have to do to hear that sound more often.

"Tell you what I'll do. I'll ask the sheriff if maybe there's a way we could keep him down at the station as a mascot, and that way Lexi can at least visit him."

"Is there any end to your generosity, Jack Butler?"

"Uh, what?"

If he wasn't mistaken, that was one adjective that had never been used to describe him. Robert maybe, but not him.

"First you want to give us your computer. You help me sort through our boxes. Then you give us a ride to church, and now you want to make sure my daughter gets her dog-fix."

While that didn't sound like him, he couldn't deny facts. "Just call me Dudley Do-Right. Speaking of which, how is your car? Any luck starting it today?"

"Nope. I'm afraid it's gone to that big junkyard in the sky."

"I can take a look at it. I know a little about cars."

What he knew about cars could probably fit on a postcard, but he didn't trust mechanics and something told him Maggie couldn't afford one.

"You know about cars, too? I was going to have Joe over on Main Street take a look at it. I can't afford much, but anything would be better than taking on a car payment."

"If I can't figure it out, you can take it to Joe's. In the meantime, how are you guys getting around?" He should have asked about that earlier.

"We walked today. One of the perks of a small town: everything is close by."

"Any time you need a ride, just let me know."

One favor had led him to another one, and suddenly it wasn't all that hard to be social again. Especially with Maggie.

Lexi had run inside her home for a towel and then dried Chief, and Jack had to admit the dog looked like a real dog. Still, the damp fur hung from him and revealed his scrawny form. Jack would probably dig through trash cans, too, if he were as hungry and desperate as Chief must have been.

"I want to finish drying him inside with my blow dryer. Is it OK, Mom?"

"I guess he can't do much damage to the house if he's in there only a few minutes and you watch him. Sure, why not?" Maggie shrugged.

"If you want to keep him tonight, well, it would be difficult for me, but I'd consider it." Jack hooked a thumb to his chest and tried more of this generosity thing on for size.

Maggie whipped her head around in the direction of her house. "Don't say that in front of Lexi. She'd take you up on it."

"The dog is good therapy for her."

That was his story, and he was sticking to it.

"Really? Well, who knows? He might make a good police dog, too." Maggie elbowed him.

"That might be stretching things a bit."

His lips felt odd, as if they were convulsing, and then he realized he must be smiling. An odd, though welcome, sensation.

"Something tells me that you also believe in lost causes."

"Also? Does that mean you're a sucker for a lost cause?"

"The lost are some of my favorite people," Maggie said. "It doesn't feel like that long ago that I was one of them."

So Maggie liked a lost cause. Without a doubt, it probably meant that she could certainly learn to love him.

Chapter 9

Who knew that a motley looking stray dog like Chief could cause a young girl an afternoon of joy? Lexi had put real effort into making Chief presentable, styling his fur using some of the hair products that Maggie used in her own hair. Later Lexi insisted on feeding him scraps from their leftovers.

Chief did look like a loving and pampered pet when Lexi was done with him and walked him reluctantly back to Jack's place late in the afternoon, complaining out loud that she wasn't sure Jack could handle taking care of a dog.

It was a good thing that Jack had pushed the lawn mower into her backyard, since Maggie required help figuring out the contraption. Somewhere in this house lay some kind of instruction manual on the machine.

In a way, she welcomed the distraction that the dog had provided, at least for tonight. It meant that she could avoid mention of Paula's phone call for a bit longer.

Sooner or later, she'd have to face letting Lexi spend more time with Paula and Richard, but for now that possibility didn't feel safe. And Maggie had to do what was best for everyone concerned. Even Matt would agree.

If anyone understood his father, it had been Matt. Richard Bradshaw thought Matt should be a lawyer, even though Matt was a born teacher. Richard didn't hide his disappointment when Matt had insisted on taking a position at a private high school in Colorado straight out of college.

"A private school?" He'd shouted at Matt. "If you insist on teaching, at the very least you'd get more money at a public school. They're union, and you'll get great benefits. Better pay, even. Where's your sense, Matt? You have a family to support."

"Their basketball team won state three years in a row, and when Lexi gets old enough to go there, we'll get a great dis-count," Matt had shouted back.

And yes, it made sense to Maggie, too. Of course, Matt could never have imagined that by the time Lexi was old enough for high school he wouldn't be in this world any longer.

Now she was a widow at thirty-one, facing spending the rest of her life alone. Slipping into bed, Maggie stared at the empty place beside her. *Lord, I feel so alone. Please help me to fill this empty place in my heart.*

It couldn't be love, a romantic relation-ship, because who would want her baggage? No, she'd have to wait until Lexi was away at college. That is, if she could ever afford to send her to college. Not likely. Maggie fluffed her pillow.

Once Lexi was grown, maybe Maggie would join one of those Christian singles matchmaking services on the Internet. But the whole thing sounded so silly and con-trived. Apparently, her pillow was the hardest one on the market since another fluff was not doing any good.

Maggie adjusted the covers a dozen times and punched her pillow into submis-sion, but sleep wouldn't come tonight. A strange occurrence for someone who had spent the past several months enjoying the escape that sleep had provided.

But today she'd been reminded that Richard Bradshaw would not give up on seeing his granddaughter again, and he'd be ready to pull out all the stops with offers of trips and all the things that would turn a young girl's head. And he had the money to do it.

Maggie pulled out her mother's Bible with the worn cover and dog-eared pages, and turned to one of the many underlined passages in Romans. Her mother's favorite, a passage she'd highlighted and underlined, Romans 8:28.

> All things work together for
> the good of those who
> love God and are called
> according to His
> purposes.

Maggie's heart lifted. It didn't matter where or what she read, the word of God calmed her and gave her peace. More than ever, she realized she had to stop distrusting Richard and start trusting God. She needed that strength now, and it wouldn't come from her own nature.

Some warm milk might help her sleep. It was two o'clock in the morning when she ambled into the kitchen and noticed a faint light coming from the front of her house. Curious, she tiptoed to the drawn shade, and lifted the edge with her finger just enough to peek outside.

Apparently, someone else couldn't sleep. Hunkered under the hood of her car stood a decidedly male figure. She could see the muscles that strained against the gray t-shirt, the long, jean-clad legs in a purposeful stance. Jack Butler, holding a large flashlight with one hand, and Chief sitting on the edge of the sidewalk as still and attentive as any guard dog.

Would wonders never cease?

"Don't start thinking this is permanent, because it's not," Jack told Chief the next morning.

Jack shook his head. Great, so now he was talking to a dog. Is that what he'd come to? Despite knowing better, it did seem to him that Chief understood him loud and clear. Otherwise, why would he hang his head and give him that hang dog, stuck- in-a-shelter look?

Thanks to Lexi, Chief now looked like a pet again, and it became clear to Jack he was definitely a Shepherd mix, one who had been at least partially trained by someone. He had a clear understanding of simple commands and had quickly learned a new one.

"Off!" had come in handy when he'd jumped on Jack's bed assuming all the warm and cozy covers were for him. Wrong.

Chief definitely had attachment problems because he'd whined last night when Jack had stepped outside to take a look under Maggie's hood. He'd thought he might as well get something done when sleep wouldn't come yet again, and Maggie had left the truck unlocked. He'd need to talk to her about that later.

Chief had seemed duty bound to come with him though all he did was sit at the curb. Then again, he probably feared losing his meal ticket again. Since Jack didn't have any dog food, he had cut up a few pieces of a leftover steak and fed it to him.

Which, come to think of it, might not be the best way to get rid of a dog.

Now, Jack opened the front door for Chief to follow. He did, as if going to work with his owner was the norm. Jack opened the passenger side door of his truck.

"I'm not an ogre, so you can sit inside now that you don't smell like a dumpster."

The dog leapt inside and sat human-like in the front seat, his body straight, his head regal. He sat in the same position the entire drive to the Sheriff's station.

What a weird dog.

At the station, Chief walked to Jack's desk and took a seat at attention.

"What do we have here?" Calhoun walked up to the dog and gave him a pat on the head.

Chief returned the gesture by licking his hand.

"Your new mascot?" Jack asked. "Mrs. Jones brought him in yesterday when you were gone and insisted that we find him a home."

"Old Mrs. Jones." Calhoun rolled his eyes.

"Thinking that Harte's Peak's finest have the answer to everything that goes wrong."

"He smelled like he'd been dumpster diving yesterday, but Lexi washed him."

"So you've got a dog," Calhoun stated.

Had all of the oxygen left the room again?

"I do not have a dog. If anything, the station has a mascot. I can't have a dog."

"Hate to break it to you, Jack, but if you don't claim that dog, it appears he certainly claims you."

Jack glanced at Chief, who now panted in his direction almost as if he'd understood Calhoun's words.

"Yeah. Here's the problem. I can't have a dog. I only brought him home to clean him up and bring him back here. You can figure out what to do with him."

Jack took a seat at his desk, causing Chief to get up, move a few paces closer and sit by his feet again. Uncanny.

"This is one smart dog. I'll talk to your landlady. My sister will probably allow for special dispensation for the dog of one of my men."

Calhoun's sister happened to be Jack's landlady, and at the time of the month-to-month agreement, the fact had been rather convenient for him. Now it appeared as though the tables had turned.

"I shouldn't ask for any special treatment. Word gets around. People talk. Carol should treat me like any other tenant." He crossed his arms.

"Nonsense. You can bring him to work with you, that way there won't be any worry about what he'd do to the place while you're gone. Unless, of course, there's a certain young teen who would be willing to dog sit."

That teen wasn't getting in his house again without someone around to watch her every move.

"Fine. I'll keep him until we find his owner. A dog like this has obviously been trained. Maybe his owners are on vacation, and they don't even know he's gone."

"Right. You do that. Until then, I'd say you have yourself a buddy."

ALMOST TWO WEEKS LATER, no one had claimed Chief, and the posters Jack had paid Lexi five dollars to put up around town had begun to fade.

Maggie hoped that the owners would not be found quite yet, even if the thought was selfish. Surely, she couldn't be blamed for loving the grin on her daughter's face every afternoon as she walked Chief around the neighborhood, took great pride in his grooming, and looked forward to the nights Jack worked the night shift, and she could bring the dog over for an overnighter.

Helping her good-looking neighbor was the least she could do even if he did have a perpetually crinkly forehead, as if always deep in thought about the trials of the world.

Somewhere along the line she'd become addicted to the softening of the planes of his face when she said, "Yes, of course, we'll keep Chief for the night."

But she wished she knew Jack Butler's story, because it looked as though it might be intriguing. Here was a striking man who spent all his time at work or helping her. He'd singlehandedly fixed her car in the early morning hours. He never had a woman around, and someone who looked like he did often had more than one.

And then there was the furniture issue. She understood the first time she'd visited him that he'd only just moved in, and there'd been one stool in the kitchen. No table, no sofa. Two weeks later, the same story. She usually brought Chief back over after the dog had spent the night at her house, and she couldn't help but notice.

If money were the issue, surely he could pick up some items at garage sales. They were held almost every weekend in the neighborhood. Even the second-hand store on Main Street had some nice furniture.

All in all, she'd have to say that Jack Butler looked as if he'd set up his life so that he could take off at any moment. And that might be a good thing for her, because she didn't care for the way her heart raced every time she saw him.

Even if he'd flirted with her, he'd only been teasing. Certainly after his experience with Lexi, he'd never want to take on their baggage. Not that she could blame him. There was probably not a man alive who would want to take them on, and she would have to get used to being alone. That would be OK, because she had the Lord.

"Mom, can Chief please sleep on my bed tonight?" Lexi asked. "I'll put an extra blanket down so he won't get on my sheets."

"I don't know, Lexi. You might be starting up a bad habit that Jack won't appreciate."

Chief sat at attention, his eyes fixed on

Lexi, as though he understood that only she had his best interests at heart. Then again, worries about spoiling him were a little shortsighted now since Lexi had been doing so from the moment she laid eyes on him.

"He won't get spoiled if it's only once. Please?" Lexi twisted her hands together in a pleading pose.

"Fine, but let's not tell his master." She patted Chief's head.

"Yessss!" Lexi gave a little triumphant jump. "Look what I taught him. High-five, Chief."

Lexi tapped his chest, and Chief raised his paw in the air to meet Lexi's.

Happy girl, happy dog. If only it could be that simple for her.

A couple of hours later, Maggie peeked in the bedroom to find Lexi zonked out, a comfortable looking Chief resting his head on her hip. His eyes lifted as if to acknowledge her presence, but he kept his head down, no doubt hoping Maggie wouldn't chase him off.

"My, aren't you cozy? You certainly came into the right home. God sure blessed you, didn't He?"

Maggie tucked the covers around Lexi

and stroked her hair. At times like this, she was able to fool herself into believing that Lexi would still be her little girl for at least a bit longer.

"Thank you for loving her."

She patted Chief's head and his dark eyes stared up at her as though he could almost understand her words. God must have sent this furry creature to give Lexi such comfort.

The doorbell rang, causing Chief to raise his head and perk up his ears.

"Don't get excited, it's probably your master home early, and I'm sure he'll be more than happy to let you stay." Maggie closed the door to the bedroom.

When she opened the front door, Jack wasn't behind it. Instead, Richard Bradshaw stood there, anger in his eyes.

Behind him, Paula pulled on his arm. "Richard, this isn't the way."

"What way is there when she won't answer our calls?" Richard's voice carried into the quiet night.

Maggie's hands shook. She hadn't seen Richard in weeks, which was the way she liked it. If he didn't quiet down, the entire neighborhood would hear him.

"What are you doing here? It's eleven o'clock at night, and Lexi is asleep."

"We're here for an answer. Paula called you almost two weeks ago about the art festival, and we haven't heard a word."

The art festival. She'd forgotten all about it, aided by the fact that she didn't want to remember. Lexi had been settled and distracted from all things related to Matt for the past couple of weeks. And she'd seemed happy for the first time in a while.

"I'm sorry. It did slip my mind." It was the honest truth, though she doubted Richard would believe her.

"Of course it did," Richard said. "You'd like to forget we exist, wouldn't you? But that won't happen."

"That's not true," Maggie stammered.

She was often at a loss for words around Richard because he reminded her so much of a bully. Her legs shook, and she stepped outside in an effort to keep the commotion from waking Lexi.

"It's not right to keep Lexi from us." Richard shook his finger.

"I didn't—I wouldn't—I..." Her voice shook.

Breathe, Maggie, breathe. Pray. Lord, please help me and give me the right words to say.

"Please, we can talk about this later. I'm sure Maggie wouldn't mind if we came back tomorrow." Paula threw her a pleading look.

"I really am sorry I forgot. There's been a lot going on lately."

"And you probably can't handle it all by yourself, which wouldn't surprise me," Richard snapped.

Maggie found the strength to shoot Richard a look of contempt even if she immediately regretted it. "I can raise my daughter without any help from you."

"You could have fooled me. What kind of mother sleeps entire days away and neglects to take her daughter to school? To feed her?"

Richard pressed at the kink in her armor with relentless drive, like any good attorney.

A grieving mother does. That's who.

"Don't say any more," Paula implored.

"I couldn't have said it better myself." From behind Paula, partly clothed in the darkness of the night, came Jack's solemn voice. "Don't say another word."

She hadn't even heard him drive up, maybe due to the sharp timbre of Richard's voice or the pounding of her own heart beat in her ears.

Richard and Paula both turned to face Jack, still wearing his uniform.

"Oh, for the love of all that is holy. Did someone actually call the cops?" Richard said. "Young man, this is a family matter."

"This is my neighbor, Richard," Maggie interrupted. "I don't know if anyone's called the cops, but you might not want to push your luck."

"Maggie is correct. I suggest you both leave now and come back at another time," Jack said.

Maggie stared at Jack who was the picture of coolness, confidence, and rock-steady assuredness. "I like that idea."

"Of course you do. Nothing like another delay. But the art festival is this weekend, and we will need an answer," Richard said.

"You can have an answer tomorrow," Jack interrupted. "One day won't matter."

"That's true." Paula again pulled on Richard.

"Let's go now, and we'll talk again tomorrow."

Richard turned to stare down Jack,

which to Maggie's mind did not appear to be a good idea.

"What do you have to do with any of this?"

Jack didn't answer, but instead moved closer to Maggie, never breaking eye contact with Richard. He didn't stop until he stood between them.

"He's—he's my friend," Maggie stammered from where she stood suddenly behind Jack.

"So now you have a gentleman friend." Richard glared. "What a fine example for your teenage daughter."

"Richard!" Paula hissed.

"I resent that implication," Jack stated in a calm voice, though Maggie swore his jaw twitched.

"Resent it all you want." Richard finally looked at his wife, as though he'd just now noticed she was there. "Fine, fine. We'll go. But this isn't over."

"Have a good evening," Jack said.

Paula rushed off behind Richard, turning once to mouth 'sorry' in their direction, and before Maggie realized what had happened, Jack ushered her inside her home and shut the door.

She managed to take in a long shuddering breath and shut her eyes. When she opened them, Jack stared at her with those blue eyes that seemed to know far too much.

"A little excitement tonight," Jack said. "So that was your father-in-law, Lexi's grandfather?"

"Sorry to say, yes."

"Piece of work, that man."

He shook his head slowly, and she noticed some of the tension remained in his jawline. She didn't like the fact that her family troubles had bled over into their friendship, but there wasn't much she could do about that now.

"I'm sorry about that. Lexi and I have caused you to bring your job home with you one too many times."

"A casualty of my job. Never really get to leave it behind."

Maggie nodded, remembering why Jack had come over. "I'll go get Chief. He's in Lexi's bedroom."

She hadn't taken one step before she felt Jack's warm hand on her arm.

"Wait."

A shiver ran down her arm, but she did not want to enter another staring contest with him now. Yet if she gazed in his eyes, she wouldn't look away anytime soon, so she refused to meet them.

"What is it?"

"What's going on here, Maggie? Why won't you let Lexi see her grandparents? Something tells me there's a good reason."

She could tell him that it was none of his business, but a strange part of her wanted to make it his business. And she needed to tell that strange and unwelcome part of herself to get a clue. She was single, and had to remain that way.

"Do you really want to know?" She didn't have to hear his answer because it seemed written in his expressive eyes. He did want to know. Somehow, he cared.

"I do."

"I don't want you to think any less of me."

He'd seen the worst side of Lexi, and he might have already made judgments about her parenting skills. What she had to tell him might cinch it.

That's why the kid is such a mess, he'd think. No wonder.

"That couldn't happen."

He surprised her by backing up, taking a

seat on her couch, and spreading his arms out. It all gave the impression of relaxation and waiting, and she had a feeling he'd be here for hours if she wanted him to be. The thought filled her with warmth.

She sat beside him. "OK. You know about Lexi's dad, but what you don't know is that after it happened I wasn't myself for a while."

"Understandable."

"I was grieving, but my way of dealing with it was to sleep. When I slept, I forgot for a while that I was alone, that my daughter didn't have a father anymore. That our whole world had come crashing down."

Jack sat, listening. No questions, only silence.

She continued. "I'm sure you've seen so much of this in your line of work. I don't know why I'm telling you this."

"Because I asked."

Right. He had a way of cutting things down to their most basic levels.

"It got to where I wasn't getting up to take Lexi to school. I slept right through entire days, waking like a zombie to force myself to check on her. She was better back then, started to cook, and even tried to get me to eat. I wasn't there for my own daughter because I was too wrapped up in my own pain.

"Anyway, Paula convinced me that the thing to do was to move back and be near them. If my own mother was still alive, I'd have come back to be with her, but as it is, the only grandparents left are Matt's parents. It seemed like a good idea at the time. I lived with them for the first few months in their mansion of a house where I felt like a warden. Paula is OK most of the time, but Richard, well, you've seen him. He's a bully. His way or the highway."

"I got that."

Yes, he'd seen a great example of that tonight. "It got even easier to sleep my grief away when Paula took care of everything. Taking Lexi to school, cooking for her, taking her to doctor's appointments. She said she just wanted to help, but I needed the kind of help they weren't giving me. And then Richard changed everything."

"How?"

If only she'd seen it coming. "He filed for custody of Lexi."

"He *what?*" Jack's eyebrows rose.

"You heard me right. Later they tried to

tell me that they wanted to do it so that they could make legal decisions for Lexi, like sign her up for school, without bothering me. They wanted to let me grieve. Get better in my own time. What they did had the opposite effect they wanted: it woke me up. I had a daughter to raise, and I could no longer afford to feel sorry for myself."

"I don't see you as someone who feels sorry for herself."

"I did for a while. The thing is, when someone so close to you is so suddenly just gone, you're left to think about every time you let them down, every harsh word spoken without thinking, everything left undone."

The light shifted in Jack's eyes, and he stared at her in silence. Somehow, he understood.

"Finally I made some phone calls and collected the small life insurance policy Matt left for us. A few days later, I bought my used car, and then I rented this house and moved us in. It isn't much, but it's home. And as it turned out, we didn't have to go to court because Richard came to his senses. He must have realized with everything I'd done he no longer stood a chance. But the truth is, I had sunk into a pit, and if it wasn't for my faith

I'm not sure I could have climbed back out again."

"I get it now. It's hard to forgive what they did to you." Jack nodded.

"I had to forgive them, but it's still hard to trust them."

Sure, she wasn't proud of it, but God knew so no use trying to hide it from Him.

"You don't have to forgive anyone," Jack stated firmly, with more sternness than she would have expected. "Some things are un-forgivable."

Maggie met his eyes because there was something he needed to understand. "Every-thing can be forgiven. No one deserves it, but that has nothing to do with it. If Christ forgave me, I think I can forgive them."

"You sound like the pastor last Sunday."

"That was a great sermon. I wish I'd un-derstood it when I was younger. Maybe I wouldn't have stayed away from the church for so long after I had Lexi."

"So what will you do? You know they'll be back tomorrow."

"I'll let Lexi decide."

Jack blinked. "Is that a good idea?"

"You haven't seen Richard around Lexi. He adores her, and she feels the same way about both of her grandparents. I don't want Lexi to feel torn between us anymore. Maybe that's why she's been so difficult lately. Lexi lost her father. I don't want her to lose the last link she has to him. Even if it makes things harder for me."

"You're amazing." He spoke the words slowly, and his eyes seemed to say the words even more than his lips did.

The compliment shook her, coming as it did from a man who didn't look like he handed them over with ease. "Oh please."

"I mean it."

I'm not the amazing one, my God is. The emotion behind those words made them catch in her throat.

She didn't imagine it when she caught Jack staring at her lips, which only made her stare at his, but instead of breaking away, she wanted to lean in closer.

But Jack rose suddenly almost as if he'd remembered he'd left the oven on, or a candle burning next door. "I've got to go."

As he moved swiftly to the front door, Maggie remembered the dog. "What about Chief? Should he stay here for the night? I'm sure Lexi wouldn't mind, and I can bring him over in the morning."

He turned to her, his hand on the door-knob and some kind of unspoken panic she couldn't decipher in his eyes.

"Sure. That would be great."

Instead of opening the door, he stood towering over her with a look of tenderness that made her breath hitch.

"Do you have to go?" Maggie dared to ask.

Yes, he does. Let him go.

His large warm hand traced the curve of her face.

"I think I do."

Maggie nodded. "See you tomorrow."

"Count on it."

Oh, she was, more than she wanted to admit.

Chapter 10

What had he been thinking? Answer: probably not much, since he'd been too busy staring at her lips. Soft, luscious lips he'd wanted to kiss, whether it was a good idea or not. And, of course, it wasn't a good idea. This was the second time he'd almost kissed Maggie, which meant he needed to get a handle on this because one thing he knew for certain.

She deserved a much better man than he could ever be. Not only that, but last time he checked he had a goal, and it was to get back to Virginia. He'd already left too many things undone, and no way would he start something with Maggie that he couldn't finish. She didn't deserve that.

But tonight, when she'd talked about her loss, it had taken him back to his own. Her words could have been his. He and Robert had left too many things undone, and too many words unsaid. And if he'd only known it would be the last time he'd speak to his buddy, he might have come up with something better to say. He ran the back of his hand over his eyes.

Jack pressed down on Robert's wound. The bullet had hit Robert in the stomach, not the chest. Had to be a good thing. There was time, still time. Plenty, and the paramedics were on their way.

Robert's eyes fluttered open. "Hey. I'm OK."

"Yeah, you are," Jack said.

"Where is he?"

Robert probably meant their prisoner, Luther Williamson, leader of the white supremacist group he'd worked hard to break up. The man guilty of the murder of a judge in Virginia. The prisoner they'd been transporting until everything had gone so wrong.

"Not for you to worry about," Jack said. "He didn't get away."

"What about the kid?" Robert asked through clenched teeth.

He wasn't fooling anyone. The sweat drops on his forehead, the pale grayish shade of his skin told the story of his pain, not that Robert would let on.

Jack didn't want to talk about the kid, and Robert had to concentrate on holding on until the paramedics got here. Which, by the amount of loud sirens he heard in the background, would be imminently.

"Don't worry about him," Jack said, forgetting that his partner could read him like one of his favorite crime paperback novels.

And where were those ambulances?

"Right," Robert spit out. "Don't worry, bro, I would have done the same."

No, he wouldn't have. Robert Craig didn't know the meaning of the word hesitate. He'd have taken care of business without a single thought. Execute. Mitigate loss of life.

The paramedics arrived, and Jack jumped out of their way. Let them work their magic. He had to call Kimberly anyway, let her know Robert was probably on the way to surgery.

There'd be one truck on the way to the hospital, one on the way to the morgue, but he only cared about one of the ambulances.

The paramedics were loading Robert on a stretcher when he grabbed Jack's arm. "Hey bud, he wants to know if I'm allergic to anything. Tell him what I'm allergic to, would you?"

In spite of himself, Jack managed to crack a

small smile. Leave it to Robert. Jack glanced at the two paramedics staring at him in expectation.

"Bullets. He's allergic to bullets."

The paramedics shook their heads and loaded Robert into the back of the ambulance. If that joke was any indication, Jack felt great relief course through his veins. Robert would be fine.

"Call Kimberly, tell her I love her and the girls," Robert said before they shut the doors.

"You'll tell her yourself. You'll be fine," Jack said.

The last words he'd ever said to Robert Craig, and he hadn't thought about them in close to a year. It was easier to forget than have to regret. Unfortunately, Maggie had forced him to remember.

Just like she forced him to feel something, when he'd tried to numb it all. And mostly he'd had success, until now. First, her kid getting under his skin, and now Maggie. Except that the way Maggie got under his skin didn't feel like a bad thing. She made his heart race in a good way. But they were a package deal, and both of them were far too much trouble.

God, I swore I'd never have anything to do with You again, but Maggie seems to count on You. So if

You're real, please make the pain stop. At least for one night.

The sound of someone pounding on his door jerked him awake, and the first thing he noticed was that the light filtering through the blinds had changed. No longer moonlight. He rubbed his eyes, but no doubt about it. Sunlight filtered through his blinds, and he'd slept all night.

Still in the jeans and t-shirt he'd changed into the previous night, he ambled to the door half-awake. The sleep felt like some kind of drug he couldn't shake off and he moved slow, almost lethargic. Strange.

"Are you OK? I don't think I've brought Chief back once when you haven't practically been at the door before I knocked," Maggie said when he opened the door.

The sight of her snapped him to attention.

She stood, wearing a green top that hugged her beautiful form and set off those green eyes.

"Sorry, must have overslept. What time is it?"

"It's nine o'clock. I would have brought him over sooner, but I took Lexi in to school late, and I thought you wouldn't mind."

Nine o'clock.

Good grief, had he turned into a banker overnight? He hadn't slept until nine o'clock since before he'd enlisted.

"May I come in?" Maggie asked.

Chief had walked right past as if he owned the place. Not good.

"Of course," Jack said and turned his head in the direction of a slamming car door. Black sedan, clearly a rental car.

No. It couldn't be, not now. But there was no denying that his past and present had just collided before his eyes. Tiny lines were now etched deeper along her dark brown eyes, her formerly long dark hair was now cut short. Still, he would have recognized her anywhere. A smiling Kimberly Craig walked towards him and Maggie.

"You can take that look right off your face, Jack Butler. I told you I wouldn't give up on this." Kimberly had an overnight bag with her, which meant she planned on staying.

Just after getting a good night's sleep, the last thing he needed. The living, breathing reminder of his greatest failure had come to visit.

"Kim—what are you doing here?" He stammered.

"Really? This is how you greet an old friend? I'm Kimberly Craig." She turned to Maggie and stuck her hand out.

"This is Maggie, my neighbor."

He introduced the two as thoughts formed and competed for attention, all of them amounting to what Maggie would think. Would she believe he and Kim were an item, or even worse, would Kim tell Maggie what he'd done?

He didn't want the look in Maggie's eyes to change when she knew. Not when she tended to gaze at him as if he were one of the greatest men she'd ever met. No need to tell her yet just how wrong she was about him.

"I was married to Jack's partner," Kimberly said, neglecting to mention why she was no longer married to him. For now, he could live with that.

"I'll let you two catch up."

Maggie left before he had a chance to think of some excuse to keep her around. And he wanted to keep her with him. She calmed him somehow, centered him. Probably because only she managed to get his mind on other things.

The door closed, and he faced Kim, who threw her arms around him and then pulled back to stare into his eyes. "I'm worried about you."

"You shouldn't be. We went over this." He felt his jaw tighten.

Kim took in her surroundings and then threw him a disgusted look.

"No couch, no table. One stool. Well, at least I can see you don't plan on staying here for long."

"That was the plan." He would need caffeine, so he headed toward the coffeemaker.

Chief chose that moment to make his presence known, pushing at his dog bowl with his nose.

"A dog? You have a dog?" Kimberly's eyes widened.

More like the dog has me. "I don't have a dog."

"Well, you could have fooled me." Kimberly bent down to pet the attention-getter. "He looks hungry."

"It's a trick. Maggie's daughter feeds him before she goes to school. Anyway, it's temporary. I'm keeping him until we find the owner."

"I'm glad. You need to come back to Virginia."

"Nothing like getting right to the point." Jack ran a hand through his hair.

"You needed a break, and I get that. Everyone does. But it's been long enough, and running away won't solve anything."

Jack set out coffee mugs and poured the coffee. "Is that what everyone thinks? That I'm running away?"

Kim took a seat on his stool. "No one is saying that. The official word is that you've taken some time off. We all expect you to be back. You and I both know it's not un-common to take time off after a—"

"Shooting?" He finished the sentence.

She shut her eyes. "It wasn't your fault, so why can't you forgive yourself?"

He had half a dozen reasons, none of which he wanted to go over with Kimberly, of all people. He'd been the one to call her, to meet her at the hospital and hold her when they'd both received the devastating news. Apparently, somehow, he was sup-posed to forget her body nearly convulsing with sobs.

All because he'd hesitated. Hesitated when he should have taken the shot, because by the time he did the damage had already been done.

He'd managed to break out in a sweat, the drops rolling down his back, and all because of Kimberly. And the memories she'd brought with her.

"I don't want to talk about this." What he wanted to hear about were the girls. Robert's pride and joy.

Kimberly talked about how they'd adjusted, Alison seeing a therapist and Amber taking horseback riding lessons, which had turned out to be therapeutic, as well. None of which, by the way, would have been required if Robert were still alive. But Kimberly refused to bring up that point.

"They'd love to see their Uncle Jack again," Kimberly said with a smile.

That would be because they didn't know, and according to the official release by the department, maybe they never would. Some things were just not fit for print.

"Yeah," Jack said, taking a gulp of his coffee.

"Do you have to work today?" Kimberly asked.

"I'll get Ryan to cover for me. He owes me."

"Great, because I have a dozen questions for you. Starting with who that beautiful woman is, and don't try to tell me she's just your neighbor."

Being grilled about what he didn't even want to admit to himself was only one step below talking about Robert. "Come to think of it, maybe I should go to work."

Kimberly laughed. "I'm not letting you get away with that. OK, I promise I'll go easy with the questions."

Great, an entire day ahead of him with Kimberly by his side. He'd have to take her for a hike, let her see the beauty of the Sierras, show her pristine Pinecrest Lake which drew visitors from all over the state.

Anything to keep her from talking.

THE MYSTERY of Jack Butler had begun to unravel itself by a single, solitary thread named Kimberly.

She'd been married to Jack's partner, but no longer. Maybe Jack was the reason they were no longer married. Except Jack didn't look like the kind of man who would break up a marriage—as if she knew what that kind of man looked like. But he wouldn't look like Jack.

If she'd had to pinpoint it, Maggie would guess that Kimberly had a good decade on Jack. Then again, some men liked older women. But now it made sense, because she could never believe that he'd be single.

Although Kimberly had said they were old friends. Then again, she and Jack were friends, and only her heart knew that her feelings had grown beyond friendship. A reminder that she had to get a grip.

A couple of hours later, Maggie heard Jack's truck start up and drive off. Probably because she'd been listening for it. Time to get busy, and get your mind off what you can't have.

Please God, help me get this man out of my mind and heart. I realize You want me to be alone now and focus on my daughter. I'm sorry about my wandering heart. I'll try to do better.

For the rest of the afternoon, Maggie cleaned like a woman on a mission. Like a woman who cared what people thought about her housekeeping habits. *I'm starting to scare myself.*

As soon as Lexi got home from school, she laid the truth out like a peace offering. "It's up to you, Lexi. I don't want to stop you if you want to go to the festival with your grandparents. Why don't you call them right now? Something tells me they're expecting a call."

"Seriously? You want me to call them? What happened to you?"

Had she been that horrible? "What happened is that God has been working on my heart for some time now. And though I'm still a work in progress, it seems as if at least the entrance has been remodeled."

Lexi continued to stare. "Is that supposed to make any sense?"

"It's a metaphor!" Maggie declared and then turned on the vacuum cleaner.

By the time Lexi returned, the living room had undergone a metamorphosis. Maggie had uncluttered and found a place in her closet for all the paperback romance novels that she tended to leave all around the house in every nook and cranny so she'd always have something to read.

"It looks nice in here," Lexi said in a conciliatory tone. "Kind of like clean."

"Thanks."

Maggie nodded in appreciation. A sense of accomplishment coursed through her. Too bad she couldn't freeze-frame the moment. Unfortunately, by tomorrow she'd need to start all over again.

"I'm going to the festival," Lexi said. "This weekend."

"I'll bet they're happy," Maggie said. "They miss you."

"You sure this is OK? Grandpa didn't believe me. He said I should ask you to be sure, and I said it was your idea. Then he said—well, never mind."

Yeah, never mind. Richard didn't usually have compliments to hand out for Maggie, but she'd been the bigger person. And, hopefully, God was smiling.

"It's OK with me as long as it's what you want."

"It sounds like fun, but I will miss Chief." Lexi shrugged as she opened the fridge and grabbed a juice box.

"Oh, thanks, honey, you'll miss a dog over your own mother?" Maggie rumpled Lexi's hair.

The doorbell rang, and Maggie opened it to find Kimberly and Jack. She definitely hadn't expected this, although she had hoped. At least her house was ready for company.

"Mr. Good Housekeeping doesn't even have a sofa I can crash on, and I won't let him take the floor. I'm only staying one night. I hope it's not too much to ask, but can I stay with you? Or I can always rent a room at the motel in town."

"You're not doing that." Jack scowled.

"Why waste money? You can sleep in my bedroom, and I'll take the hideaway bed in my couch," Maggie said.

"This is ridiculous. I can sleep on the floor," Jack said.

"Absolutely not." Kimberly shook her head.

"Maggie, the only way I'll do this is if I take the hideaway bed."

She didn't look like the kind of woman a person argued with, and Maggie nodded. "Would you like to come in?"

She took in the knowledge that Kimberly and Jack were obviously only friends and let it settle around her heart.

"I'd love to. Jack has told me so much

about this town. We went hiking today, and I got to see your spectacular lake. You're so fortunate to live in such beautiful surroundings."

Maggie gazed at Jack, who looked as if he wanted to run again, panic written all over his face. Was it something about Maggie that made him want to run? A woman could get a complex.

He sat at her kitchen table, not participating much in the conversation except for the occasional nod, glancing down at his cellphone as though he prayed it would ring.

Kimberly talked about her daughters, and Virginia, and how much they all missed Jack. But when Lexi walked in the room and said hello, Kimberly stared and then smiled.

"Jack didn't tell me you have a teenage daughter."

Maggie didn't wonder since what he had to say would not be exactly good advertising copy for Lexi. He'd obviously been kind.

"Didn't I?" Jack glanced at his phone again. "I forgot something. Be right back."

He strode out the front door with purpose, a man on a mission it seemed.

"What did he forget?" Maggie asked.

"His manners?" Kimberly laughed.

Maggie laughed, too, but she got the distinct impression that Jack was as uncomfortable today as he'd been the first time she'd met him.

"Lexi, how's school? I bet you enjoy winters here, especially if you like skiing. On the other hand, it wouldn't matter much if you didn't. Take me. I'm a first class lounger when we go to the snow. If anyone is lucky enough to get me on a pair of skis, they better steer clear of me." Kimberly apparently loved to talk, and she kept going.

Lexi alternatively smiled at their guest, and soon politely excused herself.

"She's lovely," Kimberly said.

"Thank you. I don't hear that often enough. I hate to admit it, but Lexi hasn't been on her best behavior for the past few months. In fact, she tried to break into our house because I wouldn't give her a key so she could come home right after school. That's kind of how we met Jack."

"You're kidding." Kimberly stared again.

Maggie passed a hand over her cheek, wondering if she had something on her face. "He thought Lexi was breaking in and he tried to stop her. That only made my daughter mad."

Funny how she could laugh about it now.

"I'm picturing it now," Kimberly said. "Jack hasn't been around kids that much, only our daughters. But Robert used to run a program for teenagers, and that was the first time Jack got involved with some mentoring. It was part of the Marshals' outreach to the community."

Maggie stuck on the word *marshal.* "Did you say marshal? As in U.S. Marshal?"

"Well, I'm not surprised he hasn't told you. He's not one to talk about himself. Actually, Jack is a pretty big deal in our corner of the world. Before he left, he was up for a big promotion. He and my late husband, Robert, were partners."

Well, that explained the t-shirt. In fact, it was beginning to explain a lot—from the lack of furniture to the stern authority he'd shown with Richard.

"Did you say your late husband?" Maggie asked.

"In the line of duty." Kimberly said, avoiding Maggie's gaze.

"I'm so sorry, Kimberly."

"I don't talk about it much because I'm in a good place now. Here's the thing.

Robert had a great sense of humor. In fact, he told a joke right after he'd been shot. Classic Robert. And so after the first week of bouts of constant sobbing, I could almost hear Robert's voice in my ear: 'Apparently I really was ready to do anything to avoid re-modeling the kitchen, just like you said.' You might think I'm weird, but I burst out laugh-ing. Robert would have never let me get away with feeling sorry for myself. And so now, I make it my duty to honor him by re-membering to laugh. Life is short, and soon enough we'll be together again."

Maggie wished she'd thought of that and bounced back instead of acting like the tragic widow, but the words stuck in her throat. Anyway, it was hard to get a word in with Kimberly.

"I hope I'm not speaking out of turn, but it's been tough for Jack since my hus-band passed away. Robert was like the big brother Jack never had."

Everything began to click into place for Maggie, from his attachment to the cigar to the crinkly worried forehead. Her heart hurt for Jack, a man who obviously kept his feel-ings under lock and key. He'd been grieving, just as she had, and as Lexi still grieved.

"It must be so hard. For both of you."

Maggie struggled with the right words. In her experience, words were useless in this situation, but they had to be given anyway.

"I'm only telling you this because I can see that you and Jack, well, let's not kid ourselves. Something is going on between you two. I know Jack, and I think I can tell when he's a goner for a woman."

"What makes you say that? We're friends. That's all," Maggie protested, feeling her cheeks burn.

"If you say so. Anyway, women are often the ones to decide these things. And I'm so glad to hear that."

Not exactly what she'd thought Kimberly would say, and she fought not to be offended. Maybe she wasn't the best option for Jack, but she could think of a lot worse women he could date.

Kimberly laughed. "That came out wrong. Oh, goodness, I really do have to stop talking so much. This is where I miss Robert the most. He'd give me a soft nudge, and it would be my hint to stop talking. What I meant is that Jack needs to come back home, and I wouldn't want you to get hurt."

"I wouldn't want that either." Maggie frowned.

Believe me.

"But you won't be, since, as you told me, you two are just friends. So no matter what I think Jack might be thinking, and believe me I do mean might, I still haven't managed to read his mind. There's no future for the two of you. Right? So maybe you'll help me convince him to go back?"

"Now?"

"No, not right now. I'm sure he has to give his notice at the station, give his thirty day notice for the rental. You've probably seen he doesn't have much to pack. Something tells me he's ready to leave at any moment. He just needs a little push."

Maggie swallowed. "And you think I should be the one to give him a push?"

"You're his friend, aren't you? There's one thing I know for sure: Jack won't be able to move on until he has closure. And that's waiting for him in Virginia."

"Sure. I'll talk to him, and if I can find a way I'll tell him he should go back."

Which as it so happened, was the last thing she wanted to do.

Chapter 11

Outside, Jack took a deep breath and let his constricted airway fill up.

The sun hid behind a cloud, but it was only late March. Soon the sun would be out in full force, and the last of the snow banks would be gone.

What he needed was a hike or a run, but he couldn't very well take off right now. He had Kimberly to think about, inside making friends with Maggie, telling her who knew what. He should go back inside and implement damage control, but what was the point? Sooner or later Maggie would have to know he was a failure, and maybe it would be better if it came from Kimberly.

A torn basketball net on a worn out

backboard stood on the front of Maggie's driveway. How had he never noticed that before?

Within seconds he'd run back home to get his ball, and when Chief whined for him at the front door Jack let him come out, too. Chief sat on the edge of the driveway and watched the first of several shots. The tightness in Jack's chest eased. When he glanced to the sidelines, Lexi stood next to Chief, hands thrust in her jeans pockets.

"He doesn't like it when you ignore him," Lexi said, bending to pet Chief.

"Too bad." Swoosh. Nothing but net, or at least what was left of it.

"He should be my dog, not yours. I think he loves me more, too."

"Probably right." The smug look in her eyes made him throw the ball in her direction. "Catch!"

"Wait. What?" She reacted quickly and caught the ball before it bounced.

"Hey, pretty good reflexes."

"I haven't played in a long time." She threw the ball back to him.

"Did you forget how?"

"I didn't forget, weirdo." She threw him

another one of her wish-you-were-dead glares.

"Why not prove it?" He hurled the ball back in her direction again.

She caught it and dribbled. "I used to play on a team. My dad was the coach."

"You probably know your stuff then."

"Yeah, my dad taught me how to play." She angled the ball and aimed. Didn't make the shot.

He caught the rebound. "Try again."

A few pointers and reminders and Lexi made a basket, the first of several. Once she made the first one, she wasn't much interested in letting him have the ball back.

"Just one more shot."

She threw the ball and it rolled around the rim before it fell through the net. Lexi jumped and Chief howled.

"Yes! Chief, boy, that's a three pointer. I told you I didn't forget."

"Good job. But there's no way you can do that again. Lucky shot."

OK, so maybe he wanted her to stay out here a little bit longer especially since she so closely resembled a human being for once.

The challenge did the trick, as Lexi kept at it, bumping into Chief every now and then since the dog had somehow gotten the idea that he was a player in this game.

Stopping before she took a shot, Lexi glanced at him. "Why are you out here when it's your friend inside? Shouldn't you be in there, too?"

"Maybe I don't feel like talking."

"You won't need to talk much with that lady. She does all the talking."

In spite of himself, Jack laughed out loud. Amazing that Lexi had so quickly dialed Kimberly.

"You have a point."

"I'm going to see my grandparents this weekend." Lexi said, and made the shot.

"Yeah?"

He recovered the ball and made his own shot. Maggie had stuck to letting Lexi decide, but he had to wonder if she was happy about the decision.

"So I won't be around to take care of Chief."

"He'll live."

"He'd better." She threw him a death stare. "But I was thinking that maybe you and my mom could hang out a bit."

Jack stopped mid-dribble and stared. "What?"

"She could take care of Chief for you, too, you know."

"I know."

"I don't want her to be lonely while I'm gone."

Not only did she sound human, but her voice now dripped with a word he might have never associated with Lexi Bradshaw before today: compassion.

"You don't have to worry about your mom."

He met her eyes. If there's one thing he knew about kids, it was that they tended to feel responsible for everything that went wrong. Since they were the center of the universe and all that, it was an easy mistake to make.

"I know I don't. Everyone tells me that. But they don't know her like I do. She gets sad sometimes."

"I believe you." He's seen that lonely ache in Maggie's eyes even though she did a good job of disguising it.

Lexi blinked. "Thanks. But will you do it?"

It wasn't exactly arm twisting to be asked to hang out with Maggie, and surely, the kid realized that. Was it lying when the lie was told to reassure someone? He wondered what God would have to say about that as he prepared to tell a big one.

"You're asking a lot, but if you insist, I'll hang out with your mom while you're gone."

SOMEHOW, the night passed even though Maggie didn't spend much of it sleeping. Instead, she went over and over the conversation she'd had with Kimberly. Something important had been left unsaid, but it hadn't been her place to pry. When, and if, Jack was ready, he'd tell her why he'd chosen to move three thousand miles away and give up being a marshal.

What horrible thing could he have done? Kimberly obviously didn't hold him to the same high standard to which he held himself. She saw him as the same warm person Maggie saw. A man who, if anything, might care a little bit too much.

Somehow, she was supposed to help convince Jack to go back to Virginia when for the first time in a year she felt alive again. *Lord, please help me to stop being so selfish. I need to think of what's best for Jack. Even if it's not me. Of course it's not me.*

Kimberly was also up early, and had already put the hideaway bed away and folded and stacked the sheets and blankets.

"My, you're up early. You an early riser, too? I hope I didn't wake you. My flight leaves at ten, but you know how it is at the airport. And then, of course, it's not like there's an airport anywhere near Harte's Peak. Also, I need to return the rental. All right, sorry if I'm rambling, but flying makes me nervous."

Kimberly took a breath.

Maggie smiled and started the coffee. "So you're driving yourself back. But is Jack coming over, I assume?"

"He should be here any minute. In fact, I'm surprised he's not here already. Listen, I'm sorry if I came on too strong yesterday. I get the feeling you don't want Jack to go back to Virginia after all."

Maggie started to protest when there was a light knock at the door. *Jack.*

Kimberly glanced at her watch. "Like clockwork."

Already dressed in his deputy uniform,

Jack made quick work of grabbing Kimberly's overnight bag over her protests.

"Since I can't drive you back, you need to at least let me do this."

At the door, Kimberly turned to Maggie and winked. "Remember what I said."

"I will."

There was no chance she would forget.

Maggie watched from the doorway as Jack opened the car door, hugged Kimberly, and stood, hands in his pockets, as she drove away out of the cul-de-sac. He turned, caught Maggie's gaze, and marched back toward her. Her foolish heart raced as though it had any business doing it.

"There goes one of the most stubborn women I've ever met." Jack frowned.

"She cares about you. That much is clear."

"Then I wish she'd stop caring so much." He shrugged. "Lexi told me about her grandparents and the weekend. She made her choice, I take it."

"Her decision."

Even if it made Maggie's stomach drop, she'd stepped out in faith. Uncharacteristically, she'd felt a peace about it ever since Lexi had told her.

"It was your decision first. That took a lot of guts, Maggie. I'm not sure I could have done the same."

"Actually, you helped me make the decision."

"I did?"

"You reminded me that I'd forgiven them, but my actions weren't going along with my thoughts. I had to force the two to get back in step, and it feels right somehow. I need to get her over there this afternoon."

"You do know that your daughter is worried about you." His blue eyes locked with hers, making her knees weak.

"She's worried?"

She hadn't seen anything from Lexi other than excitement at the prospect of leaving her behind.

"She asked me if I'd hang out with you so you wouldn't be lonely. And of course, she was thinking of Chief, too. You must realize she doesn't trust me with his livelihood."

Mortified, Maggie covered with a nervous laugh.

"I'll call Vera. It's not your job to entertain me."

"No, you won't call Vera. I made a

promise to Lexi, and I intend to keep it. So get ready to hang out with me today and tomorrow. I'll start by driving with you to drop her off."

He walked away smiling before she could protest anymore. Not that she wanted to, because if there was any chance she'd see that smile again she'd have to be crazy not to take it.

▭

THE HOUSE that had once felt like her prison still looked the same. Richard and Paula's large home was set back from the driveway, a wide and luscious green expanse of manicured lawn surrounded by pine trees between the circular driveway and the house. Eagle Way had been nicknamed Legal Eagle because of the amount of lawyers and judges who made their homes in this small and wealthy enclave of Harte's Peak. It reminded Maggie that the people who lived in these homes were not accustomed to losing.

And though it felt odd to have Jack with them, instead of the coldness and fear she might have expected being here again, she felt covered in warmth. God had promised to be with her, and in His grace He'd apparently sent Jack, too, like the icing on the proverbial cake.

Paula invited them in, did a double take at Jack, but welcomed him anyway. ‚Richard is just finishing up settlement talks today, so he'll be home late, but we're all ready to leave early tomorrow morning.'

A good thing, because Maggie didn't feel up to dealing with Richard today. Not after their last exchange.

Lexi raced up the winding staircase, presumably to the bedroom she'd occupied when she'd lived here.

"Your room—I mean, the guest room is ready for you," Paula called after her.

Maggie smiled at that.

Paula was trying, cozying up to Jack, perhaps to make him realize she didn't have anything against him even if Richard did. Paula took him outside presumably to show him her garden.

Maggie stayed back to stare at the oil paintings worth approximately one year's worth of her salary.

Stop judging them. Whichever one of you is free of sin, let him cast the first stone.

Oh, that's right, Lord, I'm fresh out of stones.

She could hear Paula in the garden, rattling on about the deer that crept into her garden and ruined the foliage she'd tried so hard to beat into submission. As if the deer hadn't been here first.

The last time Maggie had been in this home, she'd thought her life was over. Nothing and no one would ever make her heart swell again, and she'd have to be content with memories. But, apparently, the Lord had other plans for her.

Out of the corner of her eye, Maggie caught a glimpse of a plaque in Richard's office, the door left uncharacteristically open. Richard was private about his office, the only place he'd ever restricted Lexi from entering.

What Maggie saw glinting in the sun rays spilling in from the window had to be some kind of mistake, and it drew her further into the office as she stared at the plaque.

It couldn't be, and yet it clearly read *"Matthew Bradshaw, Teacher of the Year, Denver County Public Schools."* Maggie picked it up in her hands, turning it over. No.

The full measure of understanding hit

her like the wind on a frigid day. *The missing boxes.* Paula, after all, had helped with the packing. And while Maggie had been certain that every box had been moved into her new home, she'd been wrong about that. Matt's mementos were not missing at all. They were all here, under the Bradshaws' roof. Once again, they had taken something from her that they had no right to take.

Maggie held the plaque to her chest with shaking hands and carried it out of the office as Paula and Jack were coming back inside.

"What's wrong?" Jack asked.

He'd known her a month, and he could tell.

Paula's eyes were riveted to what Maggie held in her arms but she didn't say a word.

Maggie took a deep steadying breath. "I need to talk to Paula. Will you excuse us, please?"

She ignored Jack's questioning eyes and led Paula into the living room. Paula turned to her, eyes wide and pleading.

"Let me explain."

"I'm listening."

She didn't owe Paula anything at all, but in truth, she wanted to know. She needed to know why. *God, please give me strength and lend me the spirit of forgiveness because I cannot do this on my own.*

"You weren't supposed to go in Richard's office." Paula's chin trembled.

"I wasn't supposed to go in there and see this. What else do you have that belongs to Matt?" Maggie's voice rose while her throat constricted as though filled with sharp pins.

"It was Richard."

Paula put a hand to her head and took a seat on the couch, ignoring the fact that she'd once told Maggie no one ever sat in this room.

"How? Why?"

"When you were moving Lexi into the house you bought, I think he realized he'd lost. It hit him hardest then. He hadn't really cried since Matt died, but on that day, it hit him. Imagine what he has to live with, Maggie. He didn't accept what Matt wanted to do with his life when he was alive. When he saw the plaque, he found a pride in Matt he couldn't dredge up when he was alive."

Maggie's heart ached for Richard. He was so lost. Too lost to even know it. Hadn't she told Jack that the lost were some of her favorite people?

"Do you have everything else? I assumed

the boxes were lost or misplaced. I never dreamed you would purposely hang on to them."

"I told him he should have asked you if he might have some of Matt's belongings, and that I'd never known you to be anything but kind. But you know how he can get. I had hoped to gradually talk Richard into giving them back. Things don't replace people, and I've told him a hundred times. I have my memories, and the love Matt and I had for each other remains with me. Richard doesn't have that."

"I've been telling Lexi the same thing. Matt's mementos won't replace him." Funny how they'd both made the same foolish mistake.

"You might think that Richard is worried you want Lexi to forget we exist, but the truth is he's afraid you'll let her forget Matt."

"I would never do that."

Lexi would always have the benefit of wonderful memories of a loving relationship with Matt. They'd never wasted a moment of affection. If it were up to her she'd let Matt's parents have everything that was left of him on earth because she couldn't imagine the pain of losing a child.

"Mom?" Lexi stood at the entrance to the living room, Jack standing a few feet behind her.

"Look what I found." Maggie turned the plaque in Lexi's direction. "I guess we just forgot the boxes here. We should have thought of that."

Paula rose, and her trembling lips formed a smile.

"I'm sure we can find the rest of your dad's things around here somewhere."

"You found the missing boxes," Lexi said with a grin. "This day gets better and better."

Maggie handed the plaque to Lexi and tucked a lock of dark brown hair behind her ear. Tugging Lexi into her arms, Maggie hugged the living, breathing memento of Matt and whispered in her ear.

"Be especially nice to your grandpa today."

Lexi gave her a puzzled look, but the important thing was that she hugged back.

Chapter 12

"You want to tell me what that was all about?"

Once Jack got Maggie in his truck, he turned to her. The tension in the room had been palpable, and he'd had to bite his tongue not to intervene.

Maggie latched her seatbelt. "They had the missing boxes all along."

"On purpose?"

This had to be Richard's doing, but although the man was a bully, Jack wouldn't have pegged him for a thief.

"Richard kept them from me when we moved out. He was trying to hold on to something of Matt's, and he'd already lost his bid for Lexi."

"You're not mad." She seemed calm, at peace, but if it were him, he'd be show-me-the-punching-bag angry.

"I was for about five minutes. Now I'm sadder more than anything else. Richard is such a lost person. He has to live with the fact that he didn't love his son the way he should have, while he had the chance. None of us are promised tomorrow."

Those words hit him in the gut like he hadn't expected. His thoughts ran immediately to Robert.

"It sounds like he has regrets, but that has nothing to do with you."

"Maybe not, but I had my own regrets. I looked back and wondered if I could have done anything to affect the outcome. If I might have talked Matt out of taking that drive. Even so, I believe that all things work together for the good of those who love God. And I know Matt loved God. It's just that the story isn't over yet."

There was only one event he relived over and over in his mind. *What if?* He changed the subject, because he wasn't here to burden Maggie but to keep her busy.

"Do you mind if I take you on a drive?"

"I do have the day off."

"Then I've got something I want to show you."

Jack figured Chief would be OK at home for a couple of hours since he'd already proved himself. The dog obviously belonged to someone. Jack wondered who would have been careless enough to lose such a great dog.

He turned left on to Highway 129 and started the drive toward Pinecrest, the location of the ski lodge and a fifteen-mile drive from Harte's Peak. Though comfortably situated at a three thousand foot elevation, the altitude increased with every mile toward Pinecrest, at five thousand feet.

Small patches of snow still remained on the sides of the highway and in small melting dollops that clung to the trees even though the snow had already melted in their town.

Just before Pinecrest, he turned on to a side road. Empty land lay on both sides, part of the county's protected land. His secret place.

"This is it." He turned off the truck. "It's just a short walk."

They hiked a small distance into the woods, approaching the cavernous forest valley of trees that lay below. He saw the rock immediately, a large boulder completely out of place in these woods. It stood about four feet tall and far enough from the cliff to be safe.

Jack climbed on to the rock and offered Maggie his hand. The top of this rock offered a unique view of the wide expanse below them, and trees glistened in the sunlight as small bits of snow melted away, the only remnants of winter.

He wanted Maggie to see the beauty of the landscape, something they took for granted every day. This was the only place in which he almost felt the presence of God. *If God is anywhere at all, He has to be here. And He must be proud of His creation.*

"Wow." Maggie seemed to drink it in and smiled.

"How did you find this place?"

"I was called to help a stranded motorist who neglected to bring chains. I saw the rock in the distance, and I came back here a few weeks ago. Quite a view, isn't it?"

Maggie was also beautiful, and he'd never tire of admiring her.

"High enough to where I can see everything but not too close to the cliff where I might fall."

"Are you afraid of heights?" He didn't think Maggie feared anything but losing her daughter.

"No, I'm afraid of falling." She met his gaze and then turned her attention back to the valley.

He jumped off the rock to allow Maggie to have a better look.

Maggie took a tentative step toward the side, and he offered his hand, but in the next moment, she tripped over a crevice in the rock and fell right into his arms.

His luck might have finally taken a turn for the better, and maybe Somebody up there liked him after all. She'd literally jumped right into his arms.

"I'm sorry." Maggie's eyes were wide. "There's a reason I'm afraid of falling."

His arms filled with her, he didn't let go, grateful that she made no attempt to wrestle out of his grip.

"Listen. What do you hear?"

"Nothing."

Even though the highway was not far, at this time of day there were no cars passing by.

"That's what quiet sounds like."

"I'm not sure I like it." Maggie smiled. "In my head, I hear music."

He pulled her close and took a whiff of her sweet smelling hair, like warm vanilla sugar. Jack set her down, then framed her beautiful face and surprised himself by kissing her tenderly, her lips softer than he could have ever imagined. He was lost in Maggie again, and for a moment, he'd forgotten why he was here. He was here to keep his promise to Lexi, not to start something he couldn't finish.

"I'm glad you liked the view."

Jack let her go and shook himself back to harsh reality.

———

MAGGIE'S HEART RACED, threatening to jump out of her chest. Jack's hands felt like firebrands on her face. OK, so maybe she'd fallen a little bit on purpose, but she didn't think he realized that. And while his kiss took her breath away, now he walked toward the truck as if nothing had happened. Enough. They would have to talk about this once and for all.

"Where are we going?" She followed his long purposeful strides, trying to keep up.

"How about something to eat? There's a great place in Miwuk Village."

"Stop this, Jack. Are you kidding me?"

They couldn't ignore what had just happened between them. Could they?

"No. I never kid about food."

She didn't even smile. "You know what I mean."

"I'm sorry. I shouldn't have kissed you. I don't think that's what Lexi meant when she asked me to make sure you didn't get lonely this weekend."

"Doesn't what I want matter at all?"

Even if he hadn't realized she'd jumped into his arms, surely he noticed that she hadn't exactly pushed him away.

"I don't know why when I'm around you, I feel like I'm coming undone."

"I sort of feel the same way." She drew closer to him, as close as she dared.

"You realize this is a bad idea." He took her hand in his own. "We're a bad idea."

She thought about it. There was only one reason she hesitated surrendering her heart entirely to Jack, but she also didn't want to judge him the way she'd been judged by others in the past.

"Why?" she whispered.

"First, you have a teenage daughter who isn't crazy about me."

There was that, but she'd noticed that Lexi had softened towards him lately. She never would have pictured Lexi asking Jack, of all people, to hang out with Maggie.

"And second?"

Jack met her eyes. "I'm supposed to go back to Virginia. Although I'm not so sure about that anymore."

Maggie sucked in a breath. She was supposed to talk Jack into going back to Virginia, not give him a reason to stay. Guilt pressed down on her bones.

It's not about me, not about what I want. He needs to go back. And I need to let him go.

"Aren't you? Why wouldn't you go back?"

"For one, I like the scenery here." He gave her a meaningful look, and heat crept up her cheeks.

"Kimberly asked me to talk you into going back."

Maybe she shouldn't have come out and told him that, but her first loyalty was to Jack alone. He was the man who made her feel alive again, and maybe she could help him somehow.

"She had no right to do that." Jack scowled.

"Don't be upset with her. She cares about you, and you're like family to her. It's not fair for me to introduce my own agenda to you, but the truth is, I don't want you to go."

"Maggie," he said as he drew her into his arms.

This time when he kissed her, she twined her fingers through his hair which made him groan with pleasure. When they came up for air, they both realized they were standing by the truck but hadn't bothered to get in it. And when a passing motorist honked, it also became clear that they were visible from the road.

Jack tugged her toward the passenger door of the truck and opened it.

"We need to get something to eat and then maybe take a hike by the lake."

THIS WAS TOO EASY. Hanging out with Maggie when he'd been asked to do so, should have been a chore but, of course, he'd known better. He might not have jumped at the chance otherwise. Might have made up some excuse that Lexi could accept. The reality was that she'd asked him to do what he'd wanted to all along. He wondered if that meant that he and Lexi had some kind of truce, temporary or not. Either way, he'd take it.

"We should go back and check on Chief," Maggie suggested after their hike.

Right. He'd almost forgotten. Then again, he'd pretty much ceased to think straight for the past few hours. It seemed that every muscle in his body had relaxed and unkinked. He and Maggie were acting like a couple, holding hands as if they'd been doing it for years, and it all felt so natural.

Deep in the back of his mind there was a nagging thought that maybe he should stop feeling this way, stop acting as if he had every right to care about her. But for now, he wanted to ignore that voice and listen to Maggie's soft and lilting one instead.

As he pulled into the driveway, he noted the white van parked in front of his house, another vehicle he hadn't noticed on this street before. A couple he didn't recognize got out of the van and approached. Jack instinctively calculated the short distance between him and Maggie, how fast he could get to her, and then reminded himself to calm down. These people were not a threat.

"Thank goodness," the man said. "You're home."

"Do we know you?" Jack moved next to Maggie and slipped an arm around her.

"You have our dog I think," the portly woman said. "Our shepherd mix. We've been searching for weeks, and today we saw the sign in town."

"We don't know how it happened, but if you have our Max, he's come a long way. We live in Sonora," the man said. "By the way, my name's McGuire and this is my wife, April."

Sonora was a town thirty miles east, and it was indeed difficult to believe Chief had come that far. Then again, recalling his smell it all started to make sense. He'd obviously been on his own for some time before Mrs. Jones had found him.

"Jack Butler. And this is my…Maggie."

He walked to his front door and opened

it to find Chief standing by at attention, waiting, as he always did. As if he wasn't sure anyone would be back.

He would miss that. His own welcoming committee.

It didn't take long for it to become obvious that Chief was indeed their dog as he greeted them with his circling dance, normally reserved for meal times.

"Max, we've missed you, boy. And so have all your patients," McGuire said.

"Patients?" Maggie asked.

"Max is a therapy dog. He's been trained to work with our returning soldiers. Mostly for those suffering from post-traumatic stress disorder, that kind of thing. Max just knows when and where he's needed," April said with a smile.

"That's amazing. I want you to know that your dog has healed my daughter's heart, too. She's really going to miss him." Maggie bent to pet the dog Jack would always think of as Chief.

"Wonderful. That's what Max does. He always seems to hone in on the one person who needs him the most. And he won't let that person out of his sight usually. Maybe we can bring him back for a visit. We're not far by car anyway." McGuire nuzzled Chief's ears, and the dog leaned into the touch.

"My daughter would love that. We'll miss him around here. Won't we, Jack?" Maggie's voice seemed to come at him through a tunnel.

"Yeah."

He didn't have words as his heart pummeled in its rib cage. These people were about to take Chief away. The dog he swore he wouldn't get attached to, and now he could only think of the fact that Lexi wouldn't get a chance to say good-bye. She loved Chief even more than he did, if that were possible.

He bent down to say good-bye to Chief. For so long he'd refused to own the label, but PTSD was exactly what he'd had when he came to Harte's Peak, and this creature had somehow known. He felt a surge of gratitude he couldn't put into words.

As though he might feel the same way, Chief reached up and licked his face.

"I'll miss you, too," Jack whispered in his ear.

When he rose and glanced at Maggie, her eyes were wet.

No use in prolonging the inevitable. He and Maggie got the bag of dog food he'd purchased, the bowl, and leash. He wouldn't need them any longer. McGuire accepted them after some minor protests, and within a few minutes, Jack stood with Maggie on his lawn watching them drive away.

Maggie had both arms wrapped around his waist as though she thought he needed the support. She'd had her wits about her enough to get their name, address, and phone number so that Lexi would be able to visit. For that, he was grateful, even if a clean break was probably for the best.

Because, after all, he was going back to Virginia.

Wasn't he?

"Your thoughts are almost loud enough for me to hear them. Care to share?" Maggie asked, rubbing his back.

"I'm thinking that I'm glad you're here." He pulled her into his arms, feeling his heart rate increase. This time in a good way.

Without her, he might face another sleepless night. Without her, he feared, nothing made sense anymore. Mostly, he feared facing the truth: he was afraid he had fallen in love with Maggie Bradshaw, and that was a problem.

———

EVERYTHING MADE sense when McGuire explained that Chief was a therapy dog: the way he had attached himself to Jack and rarely left his side. Even the way he'd loved Lexi. She'd seen God at work in many ways in her thirty years, but she'd never seen him use a dog. Chief was special, but now he was gone.

And she was left wondering how she'd get Jack to tell her why he had PTSD. She had a feeling it had something to do with what Kimberly alluded to. Maggie wanted to help, but what if Jack didn't want her help? What if he pushed her away?

It didn't look as if he wanted to push her away now as he held her close. And if it were up to her, she wouldn't go any-where. Being in his arms felt so right, like the perfect fit. It wasn't supposed to hap-pen, but wasn't that the way love worked? Again, taking her by surprise. For the second time in her life, she loved a man and this time so deeply that she wasn't sure her head was involved any longer.

She'd offered to cook him dinner, but Jack was so kind that he suggested pizza for take-out, saying he wanted her to relax while Lexi was gone. All he seemed to want, maybe because Chief had left such a gaping hole, was to hold her tight.

As much as she wanted this peace, Jack had something on his mind, and she could feel it in the air between them. Somehow, she had to get him to tell her. Whatever it was wouldn't change the way she felt about him, of that she was certain.

"Will you tell me what happened in Virginia?"

Her head against his chest, she felt his heart begin to race, his chest muscles tense, and the arms that held her tighten their grip.

"Why do you want to know?"

"Maybe because Chief isn't here anymore." She raised her head to look into his eyes.

"What do you mean?"

"You may not believe this, but I think Chief was brought here for a reason. I believe that God never wastes a hurt, and you and I both know that the odds of a therapy dog winding up with the man who needed him most are pretty great."

"Maybe that's true. Chief did help me, I admit."

"I'd still like to know what happened."

"I don't like to talk about it," Jack said. "I don't know what Kim told you, but whatever it was she was out of line."

"She wouldn't say much, but she did say you need closure. You and Robert were partners, and now he's dead. I know enough to realize something terrible happened back in Virginia. Can you tell me?"

She wanted to help him, but she couldn't do it if he wouldn't tell her what he'd been dealing with. Chief had instinctively known that Jack needed help—and now it was up to her to do what she could.

Jack stood up and walked away from her embrace.

"You might as well know. I didn't mean for things to get this far between us, Maggie. You deserve so much better than me."

No, he wouldn't get away with that. She knew what she wanted, and despite the fact that she hadn't thought she'd love again, it didn't make sense to fight it any more. Her instincts about him had been right. Jack was a good man, and Chief knew that. She did too, and, she was willing to bet now, so did Lexi.

"Why don't you let me decide what I deserve? You've done so much for me and Lexi, and I want to do something for you. Please let me."

He shook his head, pacing the floor in front of her.

"If there was something you could do, I'd let you. Even your God can't help me now. It's my fault that Robert is dead. I might as well have held the gun in my own hands. He's dead because of me, and my failure."

"I don't believe that. Kimberly doesn't strike me as someone who would forgive the man who killed her husband."

"It's more complicated than that," Jack protested.

"He would have done anything for me, but when push came to shove, I couldn't do the same for him."

Chapter 13

The look in Maggie's eyes pried the words out of him. Now or never. He might as well tell her so she could run the other way. No use in prolonging the inevitable. He didn't want or need this right now, but despite that, the memories came flooding back.

"Robert and I were transporting a prisoner to Georgia's top security prison. Luther should have had the death penalty, but he had a good lawyer. Wound up with a life sentence."

"What did he do?" Maggie asked.

"He had a federal judge killed."

Maggie's face paled, and no wonder. This wasn't exactly casual conversation, and precisely why he didn't talk about his work.

"Are you sure you want to hear this?"

"I do."

He wasn't sure he wanted to tell it, but she pulled at something deep inside. "We weren't taking any chances. Luther was in shackles. It was a regular transport to the airport. We should have been home in time for the Celtics game that night."

"But that didn't happen."

"No. I heard the first pop to my left, and then Robert lost control of the van. It plowed into a fire hydrant. The shots kept coming, and we couldn't just sit there and wait to die. Robert requested backup, but we had to get out of the van. No time to discuss options. We had to seek cover. I followed the shots to a one story building while Robert sought cover behind the van with Luther. Eventually, I found the shooter on the rooftop. Alone with a sniper rifle."

"Oh no, Jack."

"The worst thing about it? He was just a kid. Luther's kid, turns out. Stupid teenager thought he'd make his father proud and stage a prison break."

Maggie didn't say a word but simply placed her hand over his wildly beating heart.

"I had my gun drawn. And I warned him. I yelled for him to stop shooting. I did everything I was supposed to do, Maggie, but I hesitated. For one second, I didn't think I could shoot that kid. But he just kept shooting, and I had no choice. One clean shot to the chest, and he was done. Too bad I didn't shoot him before he shot Robert. That one moment of hesitation cost me my best friend."

Tears filled Maggie's eyes, and he pulled her into his arms. "That's not your fault," she said on a sob.

"I hesitated. And because I hesitated, not just one, but two people are dead. Robert and Luther's teenaged son, Marcus. He was a part of the youth group that Robert led. We thought we knew the kid."

He wanted so badly to take back that day. Over and over in his mind, he'd thought of how he might have done things differently.

"What about his mother? Did she know?"

"His mother told us that her son didn't want anything to do with his father. But the truth was that she didn't even know her own kid. He'd been planning this, thought it was a way he could impress his dad. Later, we found the arsenal in his bedroom. Stupid, stupid kid."

"You shouldn't blame yourself. You did what you had to do. Who knows how many more he might have killed?"

"Yeah, I know the drill. Shoot an unarmed kid, it's wrong. But shoot an armed kid, somehow that's OK. It's still a kid who didn't get to grow up."

"I realize how you must feel, but he killed your partner. It's not like he was an innocent in all this," Maggie said.

"You want to know the worst thing about it? Robert told me he'd have done the same thing. As he was lying there before they took him to the hospital, he'd heard it was a kid. And as if he knew what I'd done, he told me not to worry. He would have done the same thing. But I second guess everything I did that day. I could have rushed him if only I was closer. But I couldn't let him keep shooting."

His hands shook, palms sweaty from the vivid memory of that day. No matter how many times he'd relived it, it still seemed to have the power to feel as if it were the first time.

"If you hadn't done what you did, even more people might be dead. I can't believe you've been carrying this around inside you. A burden like this should never be carried alone." Maggie came up behind him and wrapped her arms around his waist.

She forgave him, just as Kim had done. Forgiveness he didn't deserve.

"I've committed the worst sin. It's unforgivable, and I don't deserve forgiveness."

"But none of us deserves it. No sin is too great, because God is great enough to forgive them all."

"I can't believe that. I've put enough murderers away to know that God wouldn't have anything to do with those people. Evil to the core."

"But no one who wants forgiveness is evil to the core. And we all have sin, Jack. Do you know the Bible says that no sin is greater than another?" The sound of her voice was muffled as she pressed her head against his back.

"That doesn't make sense."

"It's true. I'll get my Bible out if you want me to prove it to you."

He turned to see the smile on her face. The warmth in those eyes had been enough to warm his cold heart, but she still wasn't done surprising him. He couldn't resist framing her beautiful face in his hands.

"Not necessary. If you tell me it's true, I believe you. Even if I don't understand it now, I'm willing to learn. In case you hadn't realized it yet, I love you, Maggie. Which is why this is so hard."

MAYBE IF SHE didn't say the words out loud they wouldn't count. But she wasn't even fooling herself with that one. She'd fallen head over heels in love with Jack Butler, but now that he'd declared he felt the same she didn't appreciate the qualifier he'd put at the end of it. And she was afraid she knew exactly why this would be so hard.

It was the reason she'd told herself that she wouldn't, she couldn't, fall in love with Jack. But her foolish heart hadn't heard a word she'd said.

Jack rested his forehead against hers, a gesture which made it easier not to gaze in his eyes. If she did he might not miss her disappointment, but of course, he had to go. It didn't mean she had to like it. Her heart raced in anticipation of the pain she knew was headed straight for her heart.

"You're leaving, aren't you?"

"I have to. It was never like me to run away from my problems, and I've let everyone down."

What about your friends here? What about me? She wanted to scream. *Not the time to be selfish, Maggie. Please Lord, help me to want what You want for Jack. If it's not me, I'll learn to live with it. I just want him to be happy.*

"I know you have to go. Remember, I was supposed to talk you into going back? I've done a bang-up job, haven't I?"

Such a great job that if he hadn't mentioned it, she would have easily let the whole idea fade into the background. She'd been so selfish.

Jack pulled her close. "Leaving here will be the hardest thing I'll ever do."

"I hope so."

That made him laugh quietly, his lips hovering so close to her ear that it made a beautiful deep sound. A sound she would miss for as long as she lived.

"If it wasn't for you and Lexi, I'm not sure I would be able to go back. You did that for me. Dragging me back to life. Knocking

on my front door, then making your way inside my heart."

"I didn't do it on purpose."

He laughed again. She was a regular
comedienne when her heart was breaking.

"You were so handsome in your deputy
uniform the first time I saw you. Even
though you did look embarrassed. I guess
I'm a goner for a man in a uniform."

"That's funny, because I'm a goner for a
woman with a big heart. And green eyes."

Maggie pulled out of his arms and took
a few steps back. He was leaving, and the
sooner she got used to the idea the better.

"You should go home now."

He blinked in surprise. But she couldn't
do this any longer, not when he'd be gone
soon. Her foolish heart wasn't listening even
now, so she'd have to give it a kick start.
Time to engage her brain. Maybe it would
listen better.

"Why?"

"You can't be serious. This will be hard,
Jack. Much harder than I can deal with right
now."

Understanding crossed his face, hard-
ening its planes again, and he hung his head,
resigned.

"I'm sorry. I'm being selfish."

"No, I'm afraid I'm the one being selfish. You're being honest."

"I can't help it if I want to spend every moment with you before I go."

"That won't happen. I can't do this. I'm a mother, and I should have guarded my heart a whole lot better than I have."

"You're not the only one to make that mistake."

He tried to reach for her again, but she moved away, a little piece of her heart protesting with a nearly indiscernible skip.

Mistake. So he agreed it had been a mistake not to guard her heart. Well, at least they were on the same page about that.

"Good-bye, Jack. It's easier this way."

"Don't do this. We're neighbors, and I'll be around a bit longer. Are you just going to ignore me?"

She would try. "We're still friends."

"But I told Lexi I'd hang out with you until she gets back. She's counting on me."

"It's OK. You've done your duty."

"Maggie, please. There was no duty here. You know I wanted to. If she hadn't asked me, I'd have found a way to come over here myself."

This wasn't working out, and he was no closer to that front door. Her throat burned and the tears weren't going to stay back much longer. The last thing she wanted was his pity.

"It's just that it hurts to be with you right now."

He winced. "And the last thing I want to do is hurt you."

Finally, he turned toward the door.

She turned her back so she wouldn't have to see him go. Within moments, the door closed. He was gone, leaving her and her wayward, aching heart alone.

Maggie picked up her cell phone and dialed Vera's number. For the next few moments, she struggled to get intelligible words out through her sobs.

"Jack…leaving…I'm…idiot."

"I'll be right over with a pint of ice cream," Vera said.

THE ICE CREAM hadn't helped Maggie much at all, but it had helped when Vera refused to leave her for the rest of the weekend. Instead, she'd called their part-time worker and offered her an extra shift.

Best of all, after watching a sad movie, Maggie had company in her tears.

"It's not fair to pull on my heart strings like that." Vera sobbed as she reached for the last tissue.

They were certainly going through them this weekend.

Even though she hadn't left the house, Maggie had peeked out the window and noticed that Jack's truck had been gone for the better part of the day. She wondered where he was, and if it were possible that he'd already left. And then she reminded herself to stop wondering. It was over.

"Do you think he'll say good-bye?" Maggie sniffed.

"That depends. How would you rate his guts on a scale of one to ten?" Vera asked, picking up the remote.

She'd rate him at an eleven, but that was beside the point. "I don't think I encouraged him to say good- bye. I ran him out of here. Maybe I shouldn't have done that."

Vera stared at her. "Don't even think about it. I know where your mind is going.

You did the right thing. Clean break and all that."

"You think?"

She was beginning to doubt everything. They were friends above all, and didn't friends wish each other the best? Once she emerged from this self-imposed pity party, maybe she'd get her own gut level up into the double digits. The Lord would help her with that.

"What do you want to do? Prolong the agony? Let him go, Mags."

"I already did."

She'd said good-bye, in fact. And no matter which way she wanted to cut it, there wouldn't be an easier or more pleasant way to say those words. Maybe Vera was right.

Once Lexi arrived late on Sunday, Maggie found the strength to put away the tears and put on her Mom hat. Naturally, the first thing Lexi had wanted to know was how Chief was doing and if he was with Jack. That's when Maggie explained about Chief's real name and his owners. To ease the pain, she told Lexi that she had their address and they could visit him anytime.

"He was a therapy dog?" Lexi's eyes widened.

"Jack suspected he'd been trained by someone. We just couldn't have imagined it was to work with people the way he does. He's a very special dog. And you knew it."

"He always seemed to know when I needed a hug." Lexi smiled, tears in her eyes. "I'm going to miss him so much."

"I'm sorry, Lex. It was hard for Jack, too. Chief wrapped himself around our hearts. We're all going to miss him."

"I wish Grandpa could have met him, too." Lexi sat with a slump on the sofa.

"Grandpa?"

"You should have seen the look on his face when he saw the box of daddy's mementos that I was getting ready to bring home. I couldn't do it. He needs to keep those things."

"You left it all there? They belong to you. Your dad would have wanted you to have them." Maggie sat beside Lexi.

"I think Daddy would have wanted me to leave them with Grandpa, and that's what I told him. He almost cried, Mom. Hugged me really tight. I carry my dad with me wherever I go. After all, he's a part of me, and I'm a part of him that isn't gone. We'll be together again one day. Don't you think?"

Maggie didn't have words. Her little girl had grown up, and come into her own acceptance of her loss with the help of the Lord.

Maggie wrapped her daughter in a hug. "Of course you'll be together again. One day, every tear will be wiped clean. It's guaranteed."

Chapter 14

"I won't accept it," Calhoun said, sliding Jack's resignation across the desk.

"What do you mean you won't accept it?"

Jack's jaw felt tight enough to lock into place. It had been seven days and three hours since he'd talked to Maggie, and Jack was in no mood.

Sure, he'd been watching her from a distance. Watching as she drove Lexi to school, and he'd even been keeping one eye on Lexi if he happened to be home in the afternoons. Every now and then, he'd drive by The Bean just to see her car there, but he hadn't been inside, letting Ryan pick up their coffees. Jack stayed away, even though all he wanted to do was hold her again.

He slid the resignation back to Calhoun.

"I'll call it a leave of absence, but your job will be here for you when you get back," Calhoun said after a long pause.

Jack closed his eyes. He hadn't expected the old man to make things harder for him than they already were.

"If that's how it has to be, but I can't guarantee that I'll be back."

"You don't have to. I can practically guarantee it myself."

"This was a temporary pit stop, until I could get my bearings. Now that I'm ready, don't make it harder than it has to be."

"Son, I don't mean to do that. I know you have to go back, because you left there too hastily. You're right that you have unfinished business back home, but something tells me that you're not done with Harte's Peak, either."

Something told him he wasn't, but a much stronger thought convinced him he wasn't anywhere near the kind of man that Maggie Bradshaw deserved. And probably never would be.

"Do me a favor? Look out for Maggie and Lexi, would you?"

"You know I will."

"Maggie's too trusting. She doesn't see the worst in people, only the best. That worked out to be a good thing for me, but she needs someone to protect her."

The fact that he'd be worried about her long distance nagged at his resolve, but he had to go back. No doubt about it.

"Funny, I thought that someone would be you." The thought had occurred to Jack more than once.

And if he'd been a better man, maybe. Well, no maybe about it. He'd be making plans to be a stepfather to Lexi, a husband to Maggie, if she'd have him. But it was all a stupid idea, and he didn't know why Calhoun couldn't see it.

"Maggie needs a good man," Jack said.

"That's right, and I'm looking at one."

"A better man."

"When will you realize that forgiveness is waiting for you if you'll only forgive yourself?"

"Are you going to start spouting Bible verses again?"

"Do you want me to?" Calhoun cocked his head.

For once, Jack wished he would. He'd misplaced, or possibly left at the motel he'd stayed in his first few days in town, the Bible Calhoun had given him. Now Jack needed a little direction. Maggie, more than anyone, had made him curious about the faith that guided her out of what had to have been one of the worst times of her life.

Jack had to start investigating, start reading. But where to begin? Should he just jump in at the beginning and read the Bible like a novel? Walking into the muddy waters of religion didn't sound like him, but for the first time in his life, he wouldn't walk away without knowing what he was rejecting.

Jack lifted a shoulder. "I'm getting used to it."

"You got it. Every time I think of you, there's one verse that comes to mind: Jeremiah 29:11. 'For I know the plans I have for you, says the Lord. Plans to prosper you and not to harm you. Plans to give you hope and a future.'"

A future. He'd almost given up on one, but when he'd gazed in Maggie's eyes for the first time the future had become hopeful.

"I like the sound of that."

Calhoun reached in his desk drawer and drew out his dog-eared Bible, the one that usually rode with them in the cruiser. He handed it over to Jack.

"I want you to have this."

"That's your Bible, and besides, you already gave me one."

"Do you still have it?"

He had a feeling Calhoun had the answer before Jack gave it.

"Uh, no."

"You'll have this one, then. It's time for me to get a new one anyway."

Jack opened the book, noting the lined passages. "But this one is filled with your notes. Are you sure?"

"That's why it's perfect for you. Something tells me you need a little guidance."

Again, the man read Jack well. Possibly one of the reasons Calhoun was, after all, in police work. He understood the human condition all too well.

"You're right. I don't even know where to start."

"For me, the fact that you even want to know where to start is good enough. Read the book, think about it, and pray about it.

Heck, investigate the facts of the Bible like you would a case. It can stand up to your scrutiny. Make sure you don't forget that it's all part of a larger story. The story of man and God is most of all a love story. And something tells me you know a little about that."

———

TEACH KIMBERLY how to operate the lawn mower.

Check.

Turned out that Kimberly used a lawn service, and that she and Robert had used one for many years.

"You, of all people, know how much my husband worked. When he was home, I wanted him all to myself. Not having to worry about a honey-do list," Kimberly had said with a smirk.

Good enough. Today was supposed to be about the grill. Turned out Kimberly had the deluxe special, a gas grill that turned on with a flick of the switch.

Jack shook his head. "You should have to work a little bit harder for fire. At least fool a man into thinking he's needed."

This was only one more reminder of how little he was needed around here, and how much he needed to be somewhere else. Back in the mountains of California, in a small town that had welcomed him with open arms. He didn't just miss the picture postcard surroundings of Harte's Peak, but its people.

One person in particular.

"This gives you more time to relax." Kimberly handed him a soda and started to line up the hotdogs.

Funny how hotdogs made him think of Lexi. He hadn't even had a chance to say good-bye. What would she think of him? Lexi had just started to warm up to him, and he'd left town. She was probably back to hating him again, if she even gave him a second thought.

Maggie was the real trouble. He woke up thinking about her, and couldn't lay his head down on the pillow at the end of the day without having her face pop into his head. She'd begun to headline his dreams, always smiling, usually singing. Never cooking. He wasn't a sadist, after all.

"How's work?" Kimberly asked, sitting down next to him at the picnic table.

"The usual." Jack took a swig of the cold soda and set it down.

"You're just like Robert. Never talk about the job."

"If I had something good to say, I'd tell you. In our line of work, there isn't anything you'd want to hear."

He caught himself referring to their line of work, as though Robert was still there. In a way, he was still with Jack every time he reminded himself to be sharp, to expect the unexpected, and never hesitate to react.

"Is it true that you're—going to church?" Kimberly's eyebrows were drawn together, in either curiosity or concern.

On second thought, he felt certain it was concern he read in those eyes. Probably thought he'd joined some kind of cult, when he'd done nothing of the sort. Instead he'd found a great group of guys at Trinity Bible Church, some of whom happened to work in law enforcement.

He walked over to the grill to check on those hotdogs. "It's true. Please don't tell me you're worried about me."

"Not worried, just hoping that it doesn't mean you're still seeking some kind of absolution."

"More like redemption."

"Uncle Jack! You're here."

Amber opened the sliding glass door to the back yard and proceeded to launch herself into his arms. He spun her around and set her down. Alison wasn't far behind, but her age showed as she went for a friendly hug instead.

"Calm down. He's staying for dinner, so you'll have plenty of time to maul him later." Kimberly got up and went inside the house, leaving him with the girls.

Alison began to rearrange the place settings Kimberly had already put out. The girl was a little perfectionist, Kimberly's mini-me.

"Are you still sick?" Amber asked.

"Sick? *Me?*" He hadn't taken a single sick day since he'd been back.

"Mommy said you're sick. Really bad," Amber said as she moved a napkin out of alignment and earned a glare from her sister.

"She didn't say he was sick, dummy." Alison, sounding ten going on thirty, frowned. "She said he was heartsick."

"Oh," Amber said. "Is your heart better now?"

Alison rolled her eyes.

Jack was transported back in time to another girl who had perfected that look.

"It's not the same thing, doofus," Alison said.

Wonderful. Overnight he'd become the kind of person whose thoughts could be read that easily.

"I'm fine," he said, turning to the sliding glass door where Kimberly stood, red-faced.

He walked to her and took the plates that she carried in her hands.

"Busted."

"Alison, would you and your sister go inside and finish prepping the potato salad?" Kimberly asked.

Once the girls were inside, Jack turned to Kimberly. "Tell me I'm not that obvious."

"I can't do that. You know I tell it like it is." Kimberly took the hotdogs off one by one, placing them on each plate as he held it out.

"By all means, please do." There wasn't anything he could do to stop it anyway.

"C'mon. I was there, and I saw the way you looked at Maggie. I saw the way she looked at you. Don't tell me you didn't notice."

He'd noticed, but there wasn't anything he could do about it when he wasn't the man he'd have to be for Maggie's sake.

"So?"

"Honestly, I didn't expect you to come back. I didn't expect her to tell you to come back. The two of you are made for each other. You both want to do the right thing despite how much it hurts you."

He hadn't thought about it quite that way, but essentially the choices they'd made for each other had led them apart. Ironic. "I would go back, if I thought I could be half the man she deserves."

Kimberly stared at him. "Really? Because from where I'm standing she'd be lucky to have you. Maggie is a beautiful woman and very sweet, too, but she's not perfect."

He lifted a shoulder. "Yeah. She can't cook. Or operate a lawn mower."

"And she probably has many other faults, too." Kimberly laughed.

Maybe he had stuck Maggie up on some pedestal where she didn't belong, but there was also the fact that he'd wanted to be a better man for himself. He'd wanted that close relationship with his Savior that

Maggie had, and if he would be any kind of a leader in a Christian home, he'd have to take those steps on his own. Even Calhoun would see the logic in that.

"I had to come back, but now that I'm back all I can think about is what I left behind. But I felt that way in Harte's Peak. Will I feel that way again if I go back?"

"It wouldn't be the same now."

He nodded. "Things are different."

The nightmares were gone, and he'd moved almost seamlessly back into the force. He'd been welcomed back with open arms and no judgment. The biggest change had come from within when he'd finally forgiven himself for having done the unthinkable.

He wouldn't have been able to do it without the Lord. These days he looked into the mirror and saw a redeemed man, a man with a second chance, a man missing only one thing.

The woman.

Chapter 15

"C'mon Maggie, it's only dinner and a movie."

"No, Vera, I told you. I don't date."

When would Vera give up? Maggie didn't want to be introduced to Vera's latest boyfriend's best friend, brother, or cousin but after two months, she still wasn't getting the message.

"That's right. What you do is fall in *love*." Vera turned the sign from 'closed' to 'open' and then faced Maggie with her arms crossed.

No argument there. Maggie didn't date, but she hadn't done such a great job of guarding her heart after all. But the man had lived practically next door, and once she'd gotten to know him, her heart didn't stand a chance. No matter. She wouldn't make that mistake again.

"All right. Point taken. Which is why I'm definitely for sure not going to date. Why take any more chances?"

She hadn't seen Jack again before he'd left. He'd obviously taken quite literally her request, her only knowledge that he'd gone being a brand new basketball he'd left for Lexi on their doorstep. A short note inside the package stated only that he hoped someday they could be friends again.

Maggie did hope so.

Her life had now settled into a peaceful, if somewhat lonely, routine. No more trouble with Lexi, thank God. No more teachers calling, and no more stealing. Who would have thought that facing her greatest fear would bring about the change they both needed?

Richard and Paula were allies now, not enemies. Lexi visited with them every other weekend, and even if boundaries were occasionally crossed, Maggie could tell that Richard was trying. In a rare and uncharacteristic moment of generosity, he offered to pay for Lexi's tuition to the college of her choice.

"Why take chances? How about because you're alive? Don't you want to feel the rush of being in love again? There's plenty of fish in the sea." Vera moved behind the counter and started to clean the espresso machine.

Plenty of fish in the sea. Yes, but none of them were Jack. And no, she didn't want to feel that way again, thank you very much. Having one's heart ripped out seam by seam was not pleasant or beautiful, no matter what the poets said.

Maggie turned toward Vera. "When I'm ready, you'll be the first to know it."

"I hope it's not too late by then."

Vera glanced up from the espresso machine but then stared at something over Maggie's shoulder. Vera's eyes widened a bit, making Maggie turn around to find out which customer had caused such a reaction.

Jack.

Heavens, he was like a GQ dream, dressed in a white button up Henley and jeans. Had he ever looked this good before? The perpetually crinkled forehead appeared relaxed for a change. His eyes no longer reflected despair, but instead simmered with something like…hope?

Maggie couldn't move, and only did so when Vera sidled up next to her and elbowed her. Hard.

"Ahem. We have a customer."

"Right. Hi. Hello. I mean, welcome back. What will it be, the usual? Of course, you'll have the usual. Americano, Vera."

She turned to shout the order to Vera, who unfortunately still stood only inches from her.

Vera winced and rubbed her ear. "Got it."

Jack smiled. "An Americano would be great, but what I'd really like is fifteen minutes with my favorite barista."

"I'm busy working. Unless you didn't mean me." She threw a glance in Vera's direction, whose forehead wrinkled in confusion.

"I did mean you, Maggie."

Of course he did. Maybe she was having some kind of a stroke. She didn't seem to be putting two and two together at the moment, but that might be because her heart was beating in time to a heavy drum solo.

Vera came up behind Maggie again,

practically shoving her from behind the counter. "The boss says you can take a break."

Maggie found herself inches from Jack now, the messy apron she wore a reminder of the first time she'd ever laid eyes on Jack Butler.

This time she remembered to remove her apron as she led him to a table near the back. Hands shaking, she pulled out a chair and sat down. Jack wanted to talk. The last time they'd talked, it was to say good- bye. He hadn't loved her enough to stay, so what was he doing back now?

She folded her hands in front of her. "So. What do you want to talk about?"

"I've missed you." He smiled, taking her hands in his own.

Her hands unclasped and went willingly with him. The traitors.

"W-what are you doing here?"

"Okay, I can see you're mad."

"That's beside the point. Are you going to answer the question or what?"

"All right, that's fair. I'm here because I'm back to stay. I got my old job back, too. Calhoun left a spot open for me. I guess he knew even before I did that I'd be right back.

Maybe because he saw the way I feel about you." His warm eyes were shimmering.

Maggie's breath hitched. Her poor old heart couldn't go there again.

"But you left. I can't go through that again. Remember, Jack, I have a daughter and everything I do affects her."

"I know. It's why I had to go away and make sure I could be the kind of man you need, the kind of leader in the home that you and Lexi both deserve. I'll be honest. I didn't think I could be. You deserve so much better than me, but I want to know if you'd at least give me a chance to prove that I can be that man. I can take care of you and Lexi."

Her resolve melted. Not a surprise because this was Jack after all, but how could she risk her heart again?

"You've changed, somehow. And it isn't just the beard."

"Do you like it?" He rubbed his chin, smiling. "It doesn't have to stay. I'll leave that up to you."

As it so happened, she thought the beard made him heart-melting handsome, not that he required any help.

"I like it."

"The real difference is inside." He let go of her hands and touched his chest. "Now I've forgiven myself, because Christ first forgave me. To do anything less than what He'd do is just stupid."

That was the difference in him, and no wonder. Jack had finally come back to God, to the place where he belonged.

Maggie swallowed the sob of emotion in her throat. "I'm so happy for you."

"I finally understand why my grandfather forced me to church all those years ago. Going wasn't a chore to him, it was a privilege. All he wanted was for me to find that joy, too, and though it took me a long time, I finally have. And it's because of you."

"Would you kiss her already?"

Maggie turned to see a smiling Ryan standing near the counter with Vera. He'd come in when Maggie wasn't paying attention, or maybe while her heart beat so loudly in her eardrums all other sounds had faded to the background.

Jack stood. "Give me a minute. I have to do one thing first."

He knelt beside Maggie's chair. "Before I left, I told you I loved you. And I meant it. Will you marry me?"

Her lips quivered so that she didn't think she could formulate a response as she stared into the eyes of the man she loved more than she'd ever thought possible.

"Yes. I love you. With all my heart."

Then Jack kissed her, more passionately than he ever had before, as though he'd left behind all the ghosts of the past. He was hers now, completely.

"She said yes, in case you missed that," Jack shouted to Ryan.

Yes. Yes to a great love again, for the second time in her life.

Yes to second chances, yes to loving without holding back, and yes to the God who graced her with more happiness than she could ever deserve.

Epilogue

One year later

Jack pulled up to Tim Whitman's driveway, and knocked on the front door. The new sheriff's badge pinned to his shirt gleamed in the sun. He'd come back to the force at a higher rank, but it was still difficult to believe Calhoun had appointed him as interim sheriff until the election. After an old knee injury had permanently sidelined Calhoun from the force just months from his official retirement, he'd asked Jack to take over. He still wasn't sure he deserved the vote of confidence.

One thing was certain: he didn't relish coming face to face with Tim Whitman again. The local newspaper had recently announced that he and his wife were now divorced, and that she'd taken Anton and the other children out of the state. Any man in his position might be unhinged, and it meant that Tim might be especially intoxicated.

The neighbors had phoned again, this time complaining of incessant banging at all hours of the night.

Tim opened the door. "What do you want?"

He held a hammer in his hands, and an acrid smell of alcohol clung to his clothes. Great.

"We got a call from your neighbors. Apparently you're working on a construction project?"

"Is that against the law now?"

Jack sighed. "It's not against the law, and you of all people know it, but your neighbors would appreciate it if you would keep to the ten o'clock curfew."

"I'll just bet you would appreciate that. Maybe make your nice new sheriff job a little easier on you. I have no wife and kids for you to rescue anymore. Do you have a hero complex, officer?"

He was goading him, but Jack was not

about to take the bait. There were no longer any brittle edges left. Just a simple, but solid, peace. He had Maggie and his new found faith to thank for that.

"It must be lonely."

Tim Whitman's eyes narrowed. "*What?*"

"Lonely. I said it must be lonely without your kids around."

Tim raised his brows. "Are you kidding? Not that it's any of your business, but I'm finally getting some work done around here. What my wonderful neighbors are whining about is the new gazebo I'm building."

Jack briefly considered what a gazebo built by a drunk might look like.

"If you need help, I know a bit about construction."

Tim Whitman burst into laughter. "I'd hire a carpenter if I wanted some help."

Tim certainly had enough money to do it. It made Jack wonder why Tim was spending the small amount of time he had off between high profile cases on a construction project he would very likely not ever finish.

"I'm sure you would. Well, the offer is there." Jack turned around to head back to his cruiser.

Tim Whitman stared after him. "Sometimes a man just has to work with his hands. Know what I mean?"

"Sure. And if that man could do it before ten o'clock at night, it would be appreciated." Jack smiled and touched the brim of his hat.

Jack hopped into the cruiser and reported in to the dispatcher. He glanced at the clock, noting his shift was over. The thought of going home to Maggie was enough reason for him to glance at the clock several times a day even though he loved his job.

He smiled, wondering how he could have ever doubted that he and Lexi could get along. She'd made him proud this year, trying out for the basketball team and becoming a decent point guard.

Maggie and Lexi grew especially close planning the wedding. Lexi was the maid of honor, pretty in a pink and white dress, but no one was ever more beautiful than his bride on that day almost three months ago.

One year ago, he'd had trouble sleeping more than three hours a night if he was lucky. These days, his bride had to rouse him every morning from a sound sleep so he wouldn't be late for work.

Even the Bradshaws were now content with Jack and Maggie's marriage, although they feigned shock when they first found out about Jack's proposal. In the end, they realized they would get to spend even more time with Lexi. She'd stayed with her grandparents while Jack and Maggie honeymooned in Hawaii and now Lexi visited her grandparents almost every weekend.

He and Maggie decided to allow Lexi to choose whether she would go back with them to Virginia when they visited Kimberly this summer. Kimberly and the girls attended the wedding, with Kimberly tactfully touting the great public schools back in Virginia. Still, he'd decided to keep their new family in Harte's Peak for now. Lexi was doing well in school and didn't need the upheaval.

Ryan teased him about his ready-made family. But when Jack saw men like Tim, he shook his head in wonder. He didn't know what he would do without Maggie and Lexi. He kissed the silver cross on the chain around his neck that Maggie gave him on the day he was baptized in front of the congregation six months ago.

There was no doubt about it. He was the most blessed man alive. Jack rolled down the long and curving driveway and headed home.

About the Author

Maria Michaels is a contemporary romance author who writes sweet, clean and wholesome books. The romances are still deeply emotional, but there's no bad language or sexual situations.

When early onset stage fright dashed dreams of Rock and Roll Hall of Fame status, Maria Michaels tackled her first novel in late 2010. She finished it in 2012, and now the fictional people that occupy her head refuse to leave.

She no longer sings unless you count randomly bursting into song to annoy her now adult children (and the dogs).

Maria lives in Northern California with her family.

Also by Maria Michaels

The Deputy's Mission

A Sweet Reunion

The Sweet Spot

Sweet on Him

A Sweet Memory

The Second Time is Sweeter

A Sweet Christmas

The Sweetest One